DREAM WORLD
DEFENDERS

KATHLEEN J. SHIELDS

Thank you Alex.

ISBN-13: 978-1-941345-23-8 Paperback
ISBN-E: 978-1-310438-85-1 Smashwords

ERIN GO BRAGH Publishing
Canyon Lake, TX
www.ErinGoBraghPublishing.com

Chapter 1

As the land sped by under Ryan's shadow he looked down from the sky in wonderment. Seeing the tops of trees, tops of hills and houses, was a unique perspective for him. He was so short he could barely see over the dashboard of his mother's car. As Ryan flew through the sky, arms stretched out in front of him, he swooped through the clouds, bursting through the fluff like a bullet. Then he dove towards the trees and swerved in and out around the trunks like a fighter pilot in a ravine.

Ryan loved these kinds of dreams. He always felt the most free in a dream like this. He could be the superhero he always wanted to be. He could be anything he ever wanted to be. Unfortunately, there was no one else in his dreams, ever. Just him, alone with his freedom; no one to save, no one to play with... no one to give him a hard time. He was okay with that, but it got lonely at times.

Soaring past the fields of corn and grain he watched as the perfect rows made patterns on the land. He dashed over to the river, where he'd make a sharp right turn and head up stream, following the curves. He looked down at his reflection in the water as he flew and smiled at the brave strong boy looking back at him. In this world, his dream world, he was everything he wasn't in real life. Oh, how he wished he could be this cool in real life!

Yet as the sun began to rise over the horizon it marked the end of his dream world and the beginning of a new day. He once turned to run away from the sun, but it followed him. He flew faster and faster, but it began to cut him off. He dodged it, flying to the right and left, but it jumped in front of him. He had been flying so fast, he couldn't stop quick enough. He threw on the brakes, shoving his feet out in front of him as if the clouds were the ground, but he slipped right through the light and popped up in his bed with the sun beaming in on him through his bedroom window.

Ryan realized, through trial and error, that when the sun came it wasn't necessarily over. He could still play for a little while longer. His world would gradually get brighter and brighter until he softly awoke to the morning sun. That, to him, was a much nicer way to wake than exhausted and freaked out.

Ryan opened his eyes and stared up at the ceiling. Head still laying on the pillow, he smiled remembering his dream, not wanting to forget the feeling of happily soaring through the world.

He groaned and rose from his pillow, swinging his legs over the edge of the bed. He put his slippers on and began to get ready for the day ahead. He was ambivalent at what the day had in store for him.

He was new in town. His parents had just moved here and it was the first day of seventh grade. He didn't know anyone which was uncomfortable, but Ryan was used to moving. Starting fresh sometimes could be a good thing. You could reinvent yourself and start over, but Ryan liked who he was. In his opinion, there was no reason to be someone different. It was just the fact that he had to show the world who he was again. Starting from scratch was the hard part. Besides, with his height, four foot six inches, and average looks, it's not like he would stand out anyway.

As he entered the school for the first time, he felt like a doodle bug sitting in the middle of an ant pile! The hustle and bustle of all of the students swarming past him made him dizzy. He followed his mom into the office where he was handed his class schedule and a map of the school and then the bell rang for class. Ryan watched as the students all disappeared from the hallways and then his mom bent down and gave him a kiss on the forehead.

"Have a good day sweetheart."

"Thanks mom." He was glad for the kiss but even more so that she waited 'til no one was around.

Ryan made his way through the empty hallway and navigated his way to class. When he arrived at the door of his first class, math, he looked in through the window at the students. Most had sat down but many were turned around talking to each other. The teacher wrote on the chalkboard. Ryan took a deep breath to ready himself, then opened the door and walked in.

Immediately, he felt about twenty sets of eyes turn to stare at him which made him want to tremble, but he kept his cool. He walked up to the teacher and handed her his paperwork. She looked at it, then at Ryan and smiled.

"Class this is Ryan Thompson from Kansas City. Please welcome him."

"Hi Ryan." They murmured. Then the teacher asked him to go find a seat. Ryan found an empty desk near the back and sat down. After he placed his backpack on the floor next to his feet, he looked up to see four faces staring at him. The questions began immediately.

"What did you do in Kansas?"

"What brings you here?"

"Do you play any sports?"

Fortunately, the teacher interrupted them to begin class and Ryan was saved from the interrogation for at least an hour.

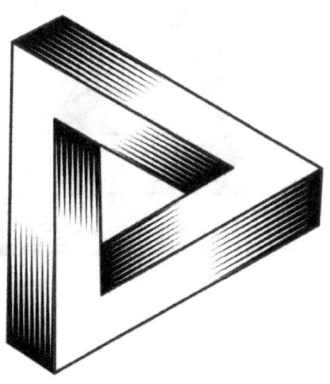

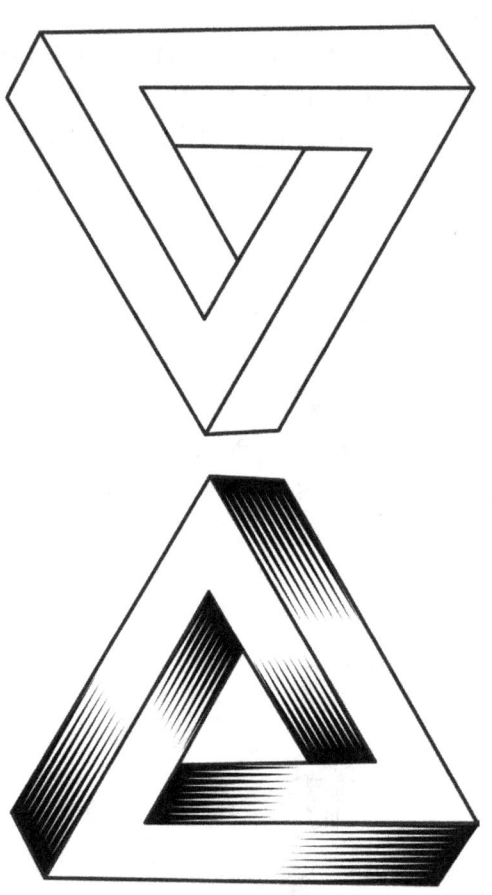

Chapter 2

Ryan got lost twice before noon, making his way into the eighth grader's hall both times. Unfortunately, his size made him stand out, big time, and a couple of the older boys made a show of saying loudly, "Hey shrimp, you lost?"

By lunch Ryan was exhausted and ready to go home, but that was when things started to change. Kaylee, a girl from his first class saw him emerge from the end of the lunch line with tray in hand and called him over to her table. Grateful for the rescue, Ryan's good humor faded as he saw that a motley crew of kids had joined her.

Kaylee's red hair was pulled into pigtails and she had a stack of books sitting next to her tray. Ryan wondered if she expected to have time to read after eating. As he placed his tray on the table to take his seat, Kaylee introduced everyone else.

"This is Owen, Parker, Blake and Justin."

Ryan nodded to each as she pointed them out and tried to memorize their names with their faces. Owen had curly brown hair and freckles on his face. Parker wore a Star Wars t-shirt and glasses. Blake had jet black hair that matched his black shirt and black jeans. Justin was tall and thin, with brown hair and dark circles under his eyes. Then Kaylee introduced Ryan to everyone.

"Ryan is from Kansas."

"Cool. Did you fly in on a tornado?" Parker asked referring to the Wizard of Oz.

"That's original." Blake groaned as he brushed his hand through his hair.

"My parents just bought this big yellow house at the edge of town."

"I know that house," Owen spoke. "It use to belong to the mayor."

"They plan on making it into a party and catering place."

"Cool." Parker spoke, "So it'll be the place to have birthday parties?"

"And weddings." Kaylee offered although none of the boys admitted to hearing her.

Justin changed the subject, turning the focus on himself. "So it happened again last night."

"Well you're not dead." Blake observed.

Parker turned to explain to Ryan who looked lost. "Justin has these crazy dreams about falling almost every night."

"Oh. Is that why your eyes have those dark circles?" Ryan asked.

"If you knew every night you took a chance of falling to your death, wouldn't you have a hard time sleeping too?" Blake voiced, looking eerily excited about talking about death as he sat there in his dark clothes.

"You know you can't really die if you hit the ground in your dreams." Ryan said.

"What makes you such an expert?"

"How do you know that?" Kaylee and Owen both spoke together.

To answer both their questions, Ryan told them the story of his dreams.

"A few years ago I began having lucid dreams. It means I am aware that I am dreaming. It didn't take much, since in my dreams I have the ability to fly."

"Cool." Parker voiced. Apparently it's one of his favorite words.

"Anyways, my mom is into these kinds of things, so when I told her about my dreams she started teaching me all about the dream world."

"The dream - *world*?" Owen questioned curiously.

"Yeah, the dream world is the place that your unconscious mind creates while you are sleeping. Dreams are the doorway into our lives. They tend to represent our deepest darkest desires or worries."

"You sound like a teacher." Kaylee spoke obviously impressed.

"My mom is like a dream teacher. She studied the subject in college and kind of interprets dreams for others. It's a hobby."

"Some hobby." Blake tried to look uninterested but was obviously interested enough to keep up with the conversation.

"She says even though dreams are make believe, there is a lot of truth to them so you should always pay attention to them."

"Truth, huh?" Blake interrupted. "I can tell you for certain I have never showed up in class naked, but my dreams put me there over and over again."

"In my dream," Owen spoke bashfully, "my teeth are always falling out."

"Every night?" Kaylee couldn't help but ask.

"No. I have all sorts of dreams, but the teeth ones kind of stick with me."

"I understand."

"Yeah, mom says we don't get anymore teeth after the adult ones come in so you want to take care of the ones you have." Justin added.

"She's just trying to get you to brush your teeth." Blake shook his head.

"Actually, mom told me about the teeth dreams. She used to have them every once in a while herself." Ryan said.

"So it's not just me?" Owen sighed with relief.

"No."

"Do you remember what it meant?" Kaylee asked wondering aloud.

Ryan thought about it for a moment. "Depending on the scenario of the dream, it can mean different things, but for my mom, it was about her worries mostly and a loss of control. Usually about work or paying the bills or something."

"How does that make sense?" Blake asked with a scowl.

"Well... the way she explained it was, your teeth are used in a smile to express your emotions. They chew your food which keeps you healthy. She says they are a sign of power. If you are losing your teeth, you are losing your power, or losing control. Either way, it means you need to do something to regain control of your life and the dreams will stop."

"You say it like you can control what you dream about." Blake scoffed.

"I can."

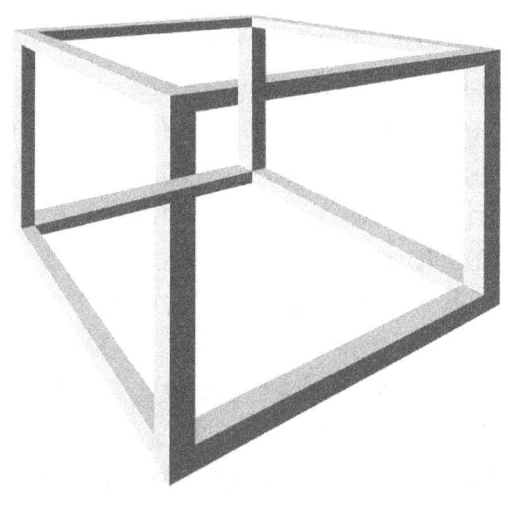

Chapter 3

"What do you mean by that?" Blake scoffed in disbelief.

"I control my dream every night. I decide where I want to go, what I want to do. I don't let the dream world control me. I control the dream world."

"Master Yoda!" Parker shook his fist in the air.

Everyone laughed, except Ryan. Kaylee saw this and asked him, "You really can control your dreams?"

"Sure, I thought everyone could."

"Do you think I'd have these dark circles under my eyes if everyone could do it?" Parker asked angrily pointing to his eyes.

"I-I'm sorry. I didn't know." Ryan spoke softly.

Kaylee, however, was intrigued. "Ryan, do you think you could teach us how to control our dreams?"

"I'm not sure. But I could try."

Just then the bell rang announcing the end of lunch. As the group got up, each thought about their dreams, wondering if Ryan could help them solve their problems.

After school, Parker met Ryan by his locker. "Okay Thompson, in my dreams I'm being chased..." Ryan looked up at Parker curiously and listened. "I don't know by who, I have never seen them, but I've been aware someone was chasing me."

"I've heard of those types of dreams. What happens next?"

"I start running! I am running as fast as I can but nothing is moving. It's like I am running in place."

"Right." Ryan encouraged him to go on.

"Well I can sense whoever it is, getting closer so I try to scream but there is no sound coming out of my mouth. I'm screaming as loud as I can, running as fast as I can but I'm trapped and terrified and then I wake up in a cold sweat with my heart racing. It's horrible!"

"I can imagine." Ryan could see just remembering the dream made Parker's adrenaline shoot up. "It's called a chase dream, and it's one of several common dream themes." Ryan could hear his mother's words tumbling out of his mouth. "Chase dreams stem from feelings of anxiety or fear in your waking life. In these types of dreams, you are usually being pursued by an attacker who wants to hurt you."

"Okay, so what do I do to keep it from happening again?"

Ryan closed his locker and they walked down the hall toward the school buses. It was nice walking with Parker so Ryan didn't have to figure out where to go. This way he could talk about this dream without the worry of getting lost, again. "Your actions in the dream, trying to run and scream, show how you would respond to pressure and cope with fears of various situations in your waking life. Instead of confronting the situation, your dream shows that you would rather run away and avoid the issue."

"Yeah, but I can't. No matter how hard I try." Parker adds.

"True, but these dreams aren't showing you what you need to see, you are being shown a situation and a response that you would give in the dream world because you haven't chosen to do something about it in the waking world."

"What do you mean?"

"The dream happens a lot, right?"

"Right."

"It is recurring - it happens over and over again. That's because you haven't done anything to change it. You have to solve the problem so it will go away."

"I try to run and scream but I can't. I wish the dream wouldn't happen at all but it keeps happening."

Ryan thought about it. "Well if running and screaming doesn't work, then stop running and screaming."

"But I'm so scared in the dreams. That's all I can think to do."

As they entered the same bus Parker stopped. "Wait! Are you on the right bus?"

Ryan looked at his paperwork. "Number three?"

"Yeah. This is three."

"Then I'm on the right bus."

"Cool." Parker took a seat and made room for Ryan to sit next to him. "Let me tell you more about my dream."

Ryan didn't mind listening to Parker. He found this an interesting subject and he was hoping he could help.

"It starts out in a home improvement store in the light fixtures section and then all of the lights go out..."

Chapter 4

Ryan was flying along the landscape enjoying another fabulous dream when he began to think about Parker's dream. After Parker left the school bus Ryan couldn't stop thinking about what Parker's dream meant. What was it that needed resolving? What did he have to do to get it to stop?

He began wondering if Parker had any idea why he was so scared in the dream, if there was going to be a way to help him. During dinner he asked his mom about it and she told him a lot that he already knew, and a little that he didn't. He looked forward to the bus ride back to school in the morning so he could tell Parker what his mom had said and to see if he had the dream again. As Ryan went to bed that night, he was still wondering about Parkers dream, recalling the terrified look on his face as he spoke about the horrid details.

It was nice, Ryan thought, to be flying carefree again in his own dream. He couldn't imagine having such a scary dream every night. It made him realize how uneasy it would make him feel, even awake, and he could definitely understand what his mom said. That your dreams not only reflect your real life, but mold you in your waking life. It's why scary dreams make scared people.

Ryan thought about this, while flying through his familiar scenery, when something not of the norm caught his attention. His world was always the same. Nothing much happens here, and nothing much changes. He was flying over a neighborhood when something in a backyard pool caught his attention. The reflected light, shimmering vibrantly blinded him at first. It was bright enough to engage his curiosity, so he flew down to investigate. As he got closer he realized there was something at the bottom of the pool. Whatever it was shined like a large diamond and refracted the light in a million different directions.

It was so intriguing and so different, he couldn't help but want to see it closer. So he took a deep breath and dove into the pool, swimming farther and farther down into the deep section until he approached the shining object. It looked like a bright hole in the bottom of the pool. As he swam closer, the light continued to draw him closer and closer until, *shwoop*, he was sucked right through.

At first, Ryan was afraid. This had never happened before. But then he just decided to go with it and, as he was pulled into the light, he found himself surrounded by air instead of water. He took a deep breath and felt himself falling toward a place he had never been before. Tumbling from an air duct out of a ceiling, Ryan fell on a cold hard floor surrounded by the brightness of a hundred lights. As his eyes focused in on his new environment, he seemed to recognize this new place.

He looked around, seeing aisles of light fixtures and ceiling fans. It reminded Ryan of a hardware store. In fact, as he examined the area closer, it *was* a hardware store, the light aisle with fixtures and displays. At the end of the aisle, he watched Parker enter the room swinging a long fluorescent light bulb like a light-saber.

"Parker?" Ryan's voice caught the boy off guard and he dropped the bulb to the floor. It shattered upon contact and made the both of them jump. Parker looked at Ryan with the most terrified look he could muster.

"It's about to happen again!"

"Your chase dream?"

Just then the lights went out and the entire place went dark. Even Ryan was a little frightened. Then, bang! The backup lights powered on and the entire area became red. As their eyes adjusted, the darkened light fixtures reflected red light that seemed to drip of blood.

Ryan looked back at Parker whose mouth was open like he was screaming. His eyes were focused down the hall, past Ryan. Parker then began running and as he ran, Ryan felt the hallway expand, stretch out of shape and elongate like some rubber band stretching. Watching this made him almost queasy. He too felt like he was being stretched. The aisle extended longer and longer. The items on the shelves blurred together until they were one single image and Ryan realized why Parker could run but not get anywhere.

Each step Parker took elongated the aisle. Each breath Parker took to scream again pushed him further and further away from reality and closer to what was scaring him. Ryan ran to Parker. He had to get him to stop running but Parker couldn't see him. Parker was too afraid. Ryan grabbed Parker by the shoulders and shook him hoping he would snap out of it.

As Parker's eyes focused on his, Ryan realized the hallway was starting to shrink back to normal size.

"We've got to run!" Parker wailed, finding his voice. "He'll be here any minute!"

"Who will?"

Parker couldn't seem to answer. Then he noticed how the hallway was almost back to normal.

"What happened?"

"Your chase dream began, but I think we stopped it."

"How?"

"Lucid dreaming – you're aware that you're in a dream so you can choose to control it. Looks like you're back in control."

"How?"

"Maybe because I am here?"

"How did you get here?"

"I don't know. This has never happened before." Ryan admitted. He began wondering about it when he felt a tugging begin to pull him. He turned to look at what was tugging him but just as he did he felt his entire body get swooped back up into the air duct he had arrived in. He was yanked through it, back into the pool, water washed up his nose and he began to choke and panic. A moment later, he was yanked back into the sky, towards the sun until he popped up from his pillow. He looked around frantically at his dark room. Once he was sure he was safe, he exhaled. "Whoah!"

He grabbed his dream journal and made notes so he wouldn't forget the way he got to Parker's dream, just in case that was some sort of a doorway.

Was I really in Parker's dream, or was I just dreaming about Parker? He noted in his journal. *How and why was I pulled back out? Was it because I began thinking about something other than Parker's dream? Did I get there just because I thought about Parker? Can I get to anyone else's dream just by thinking about them?* Ryan lay wide-eyed the rest of the night. His mother never taught him anything like this!

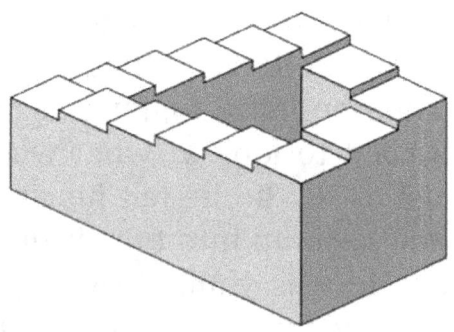

Chapter 5

"It was the coolest thing I've ever seen!" Parker exclaimed to the others as Ryan walked up to him at school the next day. "Dude, where were you this morning? I looked for you on the bus."

"I overslept. Mom had to drive me to school."

Kaylee squeezed Ryan's arm in her excitement. "Parker was just telling us how you saved him in his dream last night!"

So maybe I *was* in his dream, thought Ryan.

Blake rolled his eyes. "I wouldn't admit it if I was dreaming about someone else."

"Were you really in his dream?" Kaylee asked wondering if Ryan too had the same dream.

"So I really did enter your dream? You remember me showing up?" Ryan asked. He hadn't believed he'd been able to enter

Parker's dream, although his mom told him over breakfast that it could happen. He had never been able to do it, or rather had no desire to do it, until now.

"Yeah! And it was the coolest thing ever!"

At lunch, as soon as Ryan sat down to eat, Owen started right up with the conversation. "Ryan, let me tell you about my teeth dream."

"No way," Kaylee interrupted, "I've got to get to the bottom of my test dream."

"No way guys, I get to go first." Justin spoke. "I'm living on borrowed time. Any night, the ground could catch up to me as I'm falling and I'll die in my sleep."

"You're right." Blake asserted himself in, "Let the poor guy speak. I'm tired of looking at those dark circles."

Justin rubbed his sleep-deprived eyes, and yawned. "It's every night. Sometimes two, three times a night."

Ryan listened as Justin described his dreams. He could be anywhere, doing anything, but then he'd trip and fall and instead of falling to the ground, the ground would disappear and he'd just be falling. He would flail around in the air and scream and claw at the clouds as if they could stop his descent. And then he'd see the ground getting closer and closer and he knew. Any moment, he was going to hit and he'd be dead.

Suddenly, something would snap. He'd be yanked out of the dream to find he'd fallen out of his bed.

"Maybe it's the thought of it happening that makes you have these dreams." Ryan suggested to Justin, but Justin just shrugged his shoulders. As the bell rang, they made their way to science class.

Ryan was thinking about Justin's situation as they got to their classroom. Sitting down at his desk, Ryan looked up to see a new face standing at the front of the class.

"Good afternoon class." The substitute teacher began. "Your teacher called in sick so we will be watching a documentary today."

Ryan listened as the teacher talked about the show and while any day you get to watch TV in class is a good day, the idea of some boring documentary wasn't at all thrilling - especially since he felt so tired after loosing so much sleep last night. Before long, the lights were out. The monotone voice of the narrator droned and Ryan's eye lids were feeling heavy.

'In the rainforest, found in the undergrowth, the larvae of the...'

Ryan rested his cheek on his hand and he propped his elbow up on his desk. He yawned, his eyes began wavering and his head bobbed a couple times. He looked around to see if anyone had noticed. He re-propped his head on his elbow and it slipped across his desk. His eyes popped open. He saw darkness and heard the chirping of crickets; the documentary was still playing. As he yawned, his eyes closed. He could feel himself drifting into dreamland, unable to stay awake a moment longer.

When Ryan opened his eyes again, he was in his dream world. He smiled. He lifted off for the skies and soared through the warm day. He was always happiest here. He realized it was day time, that he shouldn't be here. Then, he began to think about Justin.

How horrible it must be to be afraid of falling to your death every night. He couldn't imagine being afraid to sleep. He was thinking deeply about Justin's predicament when he flew to his favorite apple tree. He found a nice apple as he descended and landed safely on his feet. Just as he sat to take a bite of the apple, *thunk!* Another apple fell and landed on his head.

He rubbed his head and stood up, thinking about falling apples and falling Justin's, when he noticed a dark hollow in the base of the tree. How had he never seen this before? It was so dark and seemed so deep. He looked inside, moved closer and closer, and then, *shwoop*, he was pulled inside.

The stark change of scenery, green grass to red rock, cool shade to hot sun beating against a rocky ledge was powerful. He stepped, slipping as pebbles gave way under his feet. He found himself on a narrow ledge against a solid stone wall. He cocked his head to watch the pebbles bounce off the cliff's edge, and looked down to watch them drop thousands of feet. A shadow came upon him, and he looked up to see a dark object shooting downward past him, nearly knocking him off the ledge. Within a second the sound of screaming caught up to the rapid motion of the falling object.

"Justin!"

Without thinking, Ryan leapt from the ledge and directed his flight path towards Justin. Pressing his arms against his body, he straightened, allowing gravity to pull him faster. He shot through the sky like a bullet until he caught up to Justin. He grabbed Justin by the arms, "I've got you!" Ryan yelled over the deafening sound of rushing air. He turned, and the pair soared upwards.

Looking around frantically, Justin caught eyes with Ryan. "You saved me! You can fly?!"

Ryan flew back up to the ledge and landed. "You okay?"

"You saved my life!"

"No big deal."

"It's a huge deal! Where did you come from?"

"My dream world on the other side of this mountain.

"Where?"

"Here." Ryan pointed to the solid stone wall behind him.

Justin reached and tapped the wall. "I don't get it. How do you get through?"

"I just walked through." Ryan said as he turned to demonstrate by walking through. When he came out of the other side, he turned to wait for Justin to follow but not only did he not follow, the hollow in the base of the tree was gone.

Confused and a little worried, he awoke to find himself back in class. He looked to the back of the room to see Justin with his head on the desk. He wondered if he was okay. He did leave him standing on the edge of a cliff with no where to go but down.

Ryan wasn't sure what to do. The easiest thing to do would be get up and shake Justin awake but class was still in session. He looked at the clock, fifteen more minutes left. Surely, that was enough time to go back to sleep and get Justin, Ryan thought. Just as he lay his head back down to try to go back to sleep, Justin fell out of his chair screaming.

Everyone turned to face Justin who was now awake, on the floor and beet red with embarrassment. He climbed back into his seat when the teacher walked up and whispered something to him. No doubt something like "Stay awake" or "Talk to me after class."

Ryan kept trying to make eye contact with Justin the rest of the class time, but Justin refused to look up. Finally, the bell rang and Ryan hurried over to Justin.

"Are you okay? What happened?"

"I'll tell you what happened. You left me there!" Justin began angrily. "You left me standing on the edge of a cliff. I tried to go through the wall but whatever portal you went through disappeared with you. I tried finding some other way out but couldn't." Justin pushed Ryan out of the way and headed for the door. Ryan caught up with him in the hall. "There was no way to climb up, no way to climb down. Since I was aware that I was dreaming, I tried to fly like you did, but I couldn't take off. I watched the sun set and the moon rise. I felt like I had been standing on that ledge for hours. Finally, I went to sleep on the ledge and *thought* I woke up in science class. The show ended. The bell rang. I gathered my books and followed everyone out the door." Justin stopped walking and turned to face Ryan. "Then, as soon as I stepped over the threshold I began falling, and that's when I woke up."

"Holy cow! Really?" Kaylee interrupted. She'd been following them since class let out.

Justin looked at Kaylee shyly. "It was my worst nightmare."

"I don't understand what happened." Ryan admitted. He rubbed his brow in confusion.

Kaylee put her hand on his shoulder. "We'll figure it out. The cool thing though is twice now, you've entered other people's dreams. That, I think, is the coolest thing I have ever heard."

Chapter 6

That evening, Ryan was eager to ask his mom about what happened. He found her unloading the dish washer.

"Mom…"

"Have you put your laundry away yet?" She asked interrupting him.

"Not yet. I have a question."

"You'll get it put away where it is supposed to go, right?"

"Yes. But I've got a…"

"I don't want to find those clothes shoved under the bed, or just thrown in the closet."

"Yes ma'am. But there's something I…"

"I want your shirts hung up properly…"

"Mom, can I please ask you a question?" Ryan was getting frustrated.

"Of course. What is it?" she asked putting silverware in the drawer.

"What does it mean when you wake up in a dream and think you're in real life only to find you're still dreaming?"

Annoyed to think he was changing the subject in hopes of getting away with not doing his chores, his mom spoke; "Laundry first."

"Ah, but mom!"

"Laundry!"

Ryan stormed away, stomping his feet. He grabbed a pile of his clothes, yanked open his top drawer and dropped them inside. Then he closed the drawer with a slam.

"Throwing a temper tantrum is only going to make me angry." His mother startled him while standing at his door.

"The laundry could have waited. I had an important question."

"Oh really?" His mother came back. "So I am not important?"

"I didn't say that. I said the laundry..."

"Which I worked hard cleaning, and folding and bringing upstairs, only to have you shove in a drawer."

Ryan apologized. "I didn't mean to... I'm sorry mom." Ryan went to his bed, picked up a shirt and carried it to his closet. As he placed it on a hanger, his mother spoke.

"If you want to discuss your dream while you put away your laundry I will happy to listen."

Ryan grabbed another shirt and began hanging it when he spoke, a little calmer now.

"This dream I had..."

"False awakening." His mother spoke.

"What?"

"You knew you were dreaming, were convinced you woke up, only to discover you were still dreaming."

"Yeah!"

"It's called a false awakening. It's kind of like having a dream within a dream. They can get quite repetitive if it keeps happening, especially if you don't know how to wake up."

"What do you mean?" Ryan asked. "He's never known how to wake up, it just happens." Of course he referred to Justin's dream, but he wasn't ready to admit he's been dream hopping to his mother. That would just be weird.

"False awakenings are also lucid dreams. Since you always know you are dreaming, it makes sense that eventually you would experience a false awakening. Sometimes you can get stuck in this repetitive wake-up process all night. That is, unless you know how to wake yourself up."

Ryan realized while he didn't know how to wake himself up, Justin, unfortunately did. He realized that Justin had to fall to wake up. The catch was, Justin didn't realize it or he could have woken up faster.

"Can I ask you another question?" Ryan asked as he stood by his bed.

"Will you keep putting your clothes away?"

"Yes." Ryan frowned and grabbed another shirt.

A smile spread across his mom's face. "Then what is it?"

As he hung it up he put his thoughts together. "Can you die if you dream you are falling and you hit the ground?"

His mom chuckled. "That is an old wives' tale."

"Huh?" Ryan cocked his head sideways, confused by her phrase.

"It's like a rumor, there is no truth to it. Falling dreams are fairly common, but you almost never hit the ground in the dream. Your adrenaline and fear begins to build as you are falling until you jolt yourself awake, usually by jolting yourself right out of bed. Have you had a falling dream?"

"No." He paused, then continued, "So you can't die?"

"No." She smiled.

"And you'll never hit the ground?"

"I can't say never, but I can say, you won't die."

"Well that's a relief!" Ryan exhaled as he hung his last shirt.

"See how rewarding it is to do a good job and follow it through to completion?"

"Sure mom." He rolled his eyes as she gave him a high five.

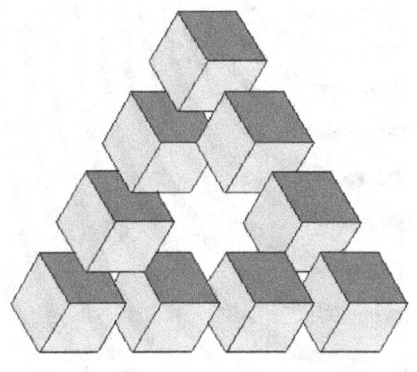

Chapter 7

The next day at school, Ryan couldn't wait to tell Justin what he found out. He was in the process of explaining everything to Justin and Kaylee when Owen walked up.

"My turn." He said as he picked at a tooth. "Does this seem loose?" He asked while leaning forward with his mouth open.

Ryan and Kaylee backed away.

"Dude, that's disgusting." Justin blocked the view of Owen's mouth with his hand. "We're not dentists."

"I'm sorry guys, but it happened again last night."

"What did?" Ryan asked.

"Owen dreams about losing his teeth." Kaylee explained.

"It is so freaky!" Owen began. "It starts out with me eating something, and then I crunch down on something hard. When I spit out what it was into my hand, it's a tooth!

Next thing I know another one falls out, and some crumble. I'm spitting out teeth. It really freaks me out."

"Freaky." Blake spoke in a sing-song voice as he walked up to the group.

Owen shyly rolled his fingers through his curly brown hair and turned to face Ryan. He whispered. "It's really scary and makes me feel like something is wrong. Like maybe I am sick and dying. I'm afraid to tell my mom because she may take me to the doctor and find out it's true."

"What?" Kaylee having listened in, spun him around. "That you're dying?"

Owen nodded his head shyly.

"You're not dying, Owen." Ryan spoke surely.

"How do you know that?" Blake asked.

"Because I've had those dreams before. They are the most common types of dreams."

"They are?" Justin asked.

"I've never had one like that." Blake offered.

"Well dreams can be interpreted in many ways. Most of the time they reflect an insecurity. Do you feel like you are embarrassed in the dream, afraid of making a fool of yourself?"

"I feel that way every day." Owen admitted.

"That is why you are having these dreams." Ryan concluded.

"Because he is afraid of making a fool of himself in real life?" Kaylee asked.

"No, because he does make a fool of himself in real life." Blake said sarcastically.

Ryan, Owen and Kaylee scowled at him. Ryan continued. "Your dreams are trying to work through some emotional problem you are experiencing in your waking hours. Your dream world has just altered the situation."

"By losing my teeth? How is that helping? If anything, that makes me feel even more insecure!"

"The trick is to face your fears. Stop feeling insecure and the dreams will stop."

"How did you stop your dreams?" Kaylee asked.

Ryan shrugged, "I dunno."

"Don't leave us hangin man." Said Blake.

"In my dreams I can fly. A few years ago, while I was in the playground for recess, I knew if I believed in it like I did in my dream, I could fly and show everyone I could do it." Ryan shook his head a little embarrassed. "So I climbed to the top of the

41

jungle gym and called everyone to watch. I was going to leap off like I was Superman with my arms outstretched. I had this big smile on my face. Everyone in the playground was watching, and I fell flat on my face. Everybody laughed."

"Dude!" Blake laughed out loud. Kaylee scowled at him again.

"So what happened?" Owen asked hanging on every word.

"I ran home crying." Ryan didn't really want to share his embarrassing story with his new friends but he thought Owen needed to hear it. "I told my mom everything and she explained what I do in my dreams is not what I can do in real life. But that didn't help my social status in school. I was ridiculed for weeks. Someone stuck a Superman S on my desk. One kid tied a cape to my chair. They called me super-dweeb and Triple F."

"Triple F?"

"Flying, Falling, Freak."

"Ooh." Justin groaned feeling Ryan's pain.

"Well that's when the dreams started." Ryan admitted. "I jumped, fell and knocked out my teeth. While in class, my teeth were crumbling. I tried to hide it from everyone but they all saw and pointed and laughed. It was tough."

"You're telling me." Owen admitted. "What did you do?"

"Mom told me what I told you. She said you have to face the kids and basically say, it happens. Once they realized I was no longer embarrassed and wasn't going to let the laughter bother me, they stopped. In fact, once I started laughing with them, I felt better about myself, made friends and the dreams stopped."

"So, what is your problem?" Blake asked turning to Owen.

Kaylee, Justin and Ryan turned to face Owen. He stared at them, unable to speak. His heart pounded in his chest. He felt their eyes boring into him, and he immediately forgot how to breathe.

Parker walked up wearing another Star Wars shirt. "So last night I didn't have a chase dream."

"You didn't?" Justin asked.

"Nope." Parker smiled broadly. "I took charge of my dream! When the lights went out in the store," he shrugged, "I just reached over and turned them back on. I wasn't afraid. No one started chasing me. I even left that dream and had another dream. I don't remember what it was about, but I remember standing up for myself.

"Cool." Owen spoke. "So Ryan, what do I need to do to stop having the teeth dreams?"

"You tell me. What are you afraid of others finding out?"

Everyone turned and looked at Owen again, putting him on the spot. Just then the bell rang, and he exhaled with relief. "Later guys," he said, rushing off to class.

Chapter 8

The next morning Kaylee rushed up to Ryan. "You've got to help me!" She urged, out of breath. Her face looked panicked.

"What's wrong? What's going on?" Ryan asked looking around to see if someone or something was after her.

"It was my dream. I was..."

"Oh!" Ryan sighed. Exasperated. Knowing there was no impending danger, set him at ease.

"I was in class, and there was this pop quiz I was unprepared for. I hadn't studied! In fact, I don't think we even went over any of the content. I looked at the test paper and didn't understand the questions, they were like written in a different language. I looked up at the clock and the hands were spinning fast. Next thing I knew, the bell rang and I hadn't filled out a single answer!"

"Okay." Ryan asked curiously, confused as to why she was so upset.

"I failed! I was unprepared. I couldn't complete the task and I got a zero on a pop quiz! It was horrible!"

"Uh-huh." Ryan stared at her.

"I can't have dreams like that."

"So you are afraid of failing?"

"Well yes."

"But it was just a dream."

"But what if it actually happens? You've been teaching us that dreams are a reflection of our real world. Pop quizzes are part of my real world. What if..."

"We've got to talk." Blake was at their side before either of them noticed. He pulled Ryan away. Ryan looked back at a bewildered Kaylee and shrugged.

Blake led him down the hall, around the corner and out the side door to the back of the school. He looked around to make sure no one could over hear. Then he looked at Ryan intensely.

Blake's size, jet black hair and dark clothes would make him quite scary if you didn't know him. Ryan was a bit anxious that he was at the back of the school where there were no witnesses with a big kid staring at him like something bad was about to happen.

"Blake?" Ryan spoke with hesitant worry.

"If you tell anyone, and I mean anyone, I will beat you to a pulp."

"Tell anyone," Ryan gulped, "what?"

"What I'm about to tell you."

"O - kay?"

"Swear! Swear you won't tell anyone."

"I swear." Ryan made the cross your heart sign over his chest.

"I was walking down the hall, heading to class, and when I walked through the door everyone was staring at me. They started pointing, laughing and then I looked down and realized I was wearing nothing but my underwear!"

"Just now?" Ryan asked dumbly.

"No!" Blake rolled his eyes. "Last night, in my dream."

"Oh." Ryan was confused. "What do you want me to do?"

"Make it stop. I keep having this dream over and over again and I am terrified it is going to happen for real."

"Has it ever happened in real life yet?"

"No, but..." Blake was caught off guard. "What does it mean?"

"It's one of those dreams that mean you are afraid of being exposed."

"Yeah duh!"

"Not like that," Ryan explained "afraid of being shown for who you really are."

"What do you mean by that?" Blake asked angrily. He moved closer to Ryan and puffed out his chest.

"Maybe you are showing people what you want them to see," Ryan took a step back, "and maybe you're afraid people will find out that who they see on the outside isn't who you are on the inside. Maybe you're hiding something."

"Like what?" Blake growled.

Ryan was a little concerned for his safety now. "Like, uh, maybe you aren't as tough as you act?" Ryan braced himself for an attack. He closed his eyes and waited. After a few seconds, he cracked open an eye to see Blake standing there thinking. "You okay?"

"You know what? I think you're right."

"Really?"

"Everyone assumes because I wear all this black that I'm a bully but I just like the color."

"Yeah?" Ryan asked, his muscles starting to relax.

"Between you and me, I'd like to try out for theater but no one looks at me and sees that. They'd think I was being a sissy or something."

"So you think others are going to judge you?"

"They already judge me."

"So you're dream is revealing your fear of people finding out that you want to be in theater. So, go join theater and your dream will stop."

"It's that easy?"

"I guess. I'm not an expert or anything."

"Thanks man!" Blake said as he gave Ryan a hug. As soon as he did though he realized the awkwardness and pulled back. "Tell anyone and I'll pummel you."

"No problem. No one would believe me anyway."

Chapter 9

That day after lunch, Blake ran over to the theater department and found the teacher. He told him about his desire to be an actor, and they talked for a while. After, Blake felt great, like a weight had been lifted off of his shoulders. He headed to gym for his next class, completely lost in thought when a couple of his friends approached him.

"What were you doing in the theater department?"

"I was joining…" Blake began before he realized who he was talking to. "None of your business."

"You were joining the theater? Are you some sissy actor?"

"No!"

"Ha - ha!" The boys laughed, "wait till we tell the guys."

Blake tried to look tough - tried to figure out how to turn this around. He watched as the guys walked into the locker room laughing. What was he going to do?

The ridicule only got worse in the locker room. There was prancing and jokes. Blake felt more and more self conscious. Gym class was even worse. They played dodge ball and Blake, who usually won, was the first to get out every time. He didn't know how to stop it.

Then, as they entered the locker room after class, it stopped.

"Sorry for all the funning we made," said one of the athletes. "It's cool if you want to do theater."

"Really?" Blake was caught off guard. "Thanks. I mean - yeah, I know."

Blake started to change out of his gym clothes when the boy began asking him questions about theater. They talked about theater and acting, and Blake got excited. He didn't hear the first bell as the two of them continued talking. Two minutes later, the boy said a quick "See ya later" and ran off leaving Blake tying his shoes.

When the bell rang for the second time, Blake suddenly realized he was late for class. Surprised that he was the only one left in the locker room, he panicked. He slammed his locker shut and ran out the door as fast as he could. He sprinted down the hall and into his next class that was already in session.

As he burst through the door, everyone turned to stare at him. Then a few started pointing while others began laughing. Blake didn't know being late to class was such a big deal.

"Polka dots!" someone laughed and pointed. Blake's heart sank. He looked down and saw his purple polka dot underwear and realized he forgot to put his shorts on after gym. He had tied his shoes, gotten his shirt but completely forgot his shorts.

It was his dream in real life!

The noise in the classroom went from giggles and chuckles to whoops and cries of laughter. Blake couldn't help but turn and run out of the room as fast as he could. He ran down the hall, to the gym, burst into the locker room and into the shower stalls and collapsed onto the floor.

He couldn't believe it. His worst nightmare had come true. He was devastated, embarrassed and growing angry. This all happened because of Ryan. Ryan said if he faced his fears he'd stop having these dreams. He never said anything about the dreams happening in real life. He'd trusted him. Growing angrier by the minute Blake grabbed his gym shorts from his locker and made his way down the hall to Ryan's class.

Blake waited outside the door for the bell to ring. When Ryan came out of the room, Blake grabbed him by the shirt collar and threw him up against the lockers.

"This is all YOUR fault!"

Ryan was confused. One moment he was walking out of class trying to stay awake, the next he had been thrown up against the lockers and everyone surrounded them chanting the word, fight.

"What did I do?"

"You made it happen. I did what you said, and it happened."

"What?" Ryan squeaked.

"My worst nightmare, that's what!"

"You walked into class naked?"

Everyone began laughing. Blake threw his fist into the locker next to Ryan's head. "This is your fault!"

"How is it my fault? I wasn't anywhere around you."

Just then, the boy from the locker room walked up. He'd heard about Blake's misfortune. "Good to see you found some shorts," he said with a smirk.

Blake spun around to face him. The boy held Blake's shorts up for everyone to see.

All of a sudden, Blake realized why he'd forgotten to put on his shorts. He had been preoccupied talking to the boy. He must have planned it. He'd taken Blake's shorts when he left the locker room.

Now Blake realized it had nothing to do with Ryan. He walked up to the boy and snatched his shorts out of his hands. "Thief!"

Just then, a teacher interrupted the scene. "What is going on here?"

No one spoke, but Ryan knew Blake needed help. "That kid stole Blake's shorts and was taunting him."

The teacher turned to the boy and scowled. "Theft will not be tolerated in this school." She took him by the arm and hauled him down the hall to the principal's office. The crowd began to disburse.

"Thanks for not squealin' on me."

"Thanks for not beatin' me up."

"Sorry I threw you against the lockers." Blake apologized.

"I'm sorry you had such a bad experience." Ryan admitted.

Both boys just stood there for a moment staring at each other.

"So how about that game last night?" Ryan broke the silence.

"Yeah that was a great game."

The two of them walked away like nothing had happened.

Chapter 10

Kaylee had been forming an idea all week, that she was desperate to try out. She had been researching dreams, especially lucid dreaming. Ever since she met Ryan and learned that he could jump into dreams, her imagination had run wild. She couldn't help but envision the possibilities. She'd tried to jump into someone else's dreams throughout the week but hadn't been able to do it. She had even tried having her own lucid dreams but she hadn't been successful in controlling her dreams either.

After hearing about everyone's experiences, especially how Justin became aware of his dream, she decided it was all connected to Ryan's arrival. Even Parker was able to control his dream after Ryan visited him. Kaylee realized, if she was going to get down to the bottom of her dream, she'd have to have Ryan enter hers. But she also wanted to take it a step farther.

What Kaylee wanted was to get everyone together in one dream. Why should Ryan be the only one who could visit? Why should Ryan be the only one who could fly? Why couldn't they all control their dreams and have adventures together?

She made lists, wrote down details and left blanks where she needed additional information. Then, when she was ready, she gathered the boys to declare her plan.

"Who here wants to fly?"

They all kind of nodded. They knew there was no real way to fly so Kaylee had to have been talking about something imaginary.

"What if I told you I could make it happen... with Ryan's help."

The boys were intrigued, especially Ryan who had no idea what she wanted, but apparently played a special role in her plan.

"I believe, with all the right details, with all the right preparation, we could not only become aware of our dreams, but all get together in one dream and fly."

Parker was definitely interested. He had already experienced Ryan enter his dreams. He had been able to have lucid dreams ever since. He hadn't mastered flying but he had been aware when he was dreaming. It was an excellent start. "I'm in."

Kaylee continued. "Ryan was able to enter Parker's dream because Parker described exactly where he was and what happened. He did the same for Justin."

"That's right." Justin spoke, "But he left me. He said I could walk right through the wall but I couldn't."

"Did you believe you could walk through the wall when he said it?" Kaylee asked.

"No. Of course not."

"That's why." Ryan added. "You have to believe it. Then it can happen."

"So are you saying, we all can do it?"

"I'm saying I want to try. Do you?" She looked around at the boys. They all nodded their heads.

"What do we need to do?"

"Meet me after school at the public library."

That afternoon they all described their dreams in detail. Owen, Blake and Kaylee's dreams were easy, they all took place in school. Ryan concluded the easiest thing to do would be to enter Parker's and Justin's dreams first, then bring them to the school where they would enter the other's dreams. Then, it would be up to him to figure out how to get back to his world with them.

"So how did you find Parker?"

"I followed a shimmering light at the bottom of a pool. It sucked me through a porthole into the home improvement store's light fixture aisle. And then with Justin, it was the knot hole in the base of the apple tree. That dropped me at the cliffs edge."

"But I've never gotten to the school, and I don't know what that hidden entrance would be. I didn't even know the other anomalies would take me to them."

Kaylee thought about it for a moment. "Had you been thinking about Parker in the light aisle?"

"I think so."

"And when you were sitting by the apple tree, did you think about Justin at the cliff's edge?"

"Yes. But I don't understand the connection. A hole in the base of a tree is not like a cliff on the side of a mountain."

"That is, until you take into consideration the fact that it appeared right after you thought about him."

"And that it was a shimmery light that led you to a light aisle."

"Okay, but that still doesn't help me get into the school."

"True, but we are going to figure that out right now."

"How?"

"What pops into your head first when you think about school?"

"The bell ringing."

"There you go." Kaylee said matter-of-factly.

"What?"

"After you get Parker and Justin, think about one of us at school and where ever you hear the school bell is where you need to go."

"Makes sense, I think, but I still don't understand..."

"You'll figure it out. Just like you figured out the others. It will be something you've never seen in your world and you'll figure out how to get through it."

"Okay. I'll do it. How do we proceed?"

"Okay, so here is the plan..."

Chapter 11

That night before Ryan went to sleep, he looked over the notes Kaylee had made for each of them and memorized each scene. The others had been instructed to do the same. When Ryan awoke in his dream world, he flew over to the apple orchard so he could get Justin.

Justin planned to think about falling until he fell asleep so he could fall in his dream. He only hoped Ryan would be there to catch him, because the big debate this afternoon went like this:

"But if I am aware I am dreaming and lucid enough to force myself to fall, then it stands to reason that if I hit the ground I truly will die and be aware of it even."

"But if you are having a lucid dream and are aware of it, then you can keep yourself from falling or stop your fall before you die. You may even be able to land on your feet, even if you can't control flight."

Even though Justin was hesitant, he planned on going first.

Ryan found the tree, thought about Justin and smiled when the hole appeared. He immediately walked through but knew he had to be cautious to not walk right over the edge. As he stepped out, the world again caught him off guard. It was so hot and so bright. The sun was just beating on the rock of the cliff and radiating like an oven. Ryan almost immediately began to sweat.

His eyes hadn't yet grown accustomed to the light, but he heard the familiar sound of Justin screaming above him getting louder by the moment.

Squinting, Ryan watched as Justin fell toward him, barreling from the sky like an out of control airplane. As he got closer, Ryan yelled up to him.

"Justin! I'm here!"

Justin looked down to see Ryan perched on the ledge. Justin twisted in the air until his feet were facing down. Then, with the power of Superman, he landed right next to Ryan on the ledge. Ryan was truly impressed. Justin had taken control of his dream.

"Ready?" Ryan asked with a smile.

"Yes!" Justin said proudly. "I am!"

Taking Justin's hand in his, Ryan pulled Justin through the wall with a long, drawn out, shwoooo-oop. He turned to look at Justin's reaction as he entered Ryan's world.

"This is amazing!" Justin spoke with eyes opened wide. He looked back at the hole on the apple tree and watched it disappear. "How will I get back?"

"Hopefully, you won't need to get back. You can go anywhere you want, why would you want to return to a place where you are always falling?"

"Good point." Justin said as he looked around Ryan's world. It was beautiful, colorful and calm, like a scene out of a magazine. A quiet countryside with rolling green hills, butterflies and birds singing. There was a light breeze and the temperature was way more pleasant than the hot desert climate Justin was used to in his dream.

"All right," Ryan clapped his hands together. "Ready for your first flying lesson?"

"Definitely! How do we begin?"

"I don't know. I just take off." He said as he pushed off with his feet and shot up into the sky. Slowing, then turning back towards Justin, Ryan spoke. "Just jump."

Justin jumped up into the air but gravity yanked him back down. He leaped again, and landed. He squatted down and shot up with his legs as hard as he could but he landed back down on the ground again. "It's not working."

Ryan thought about it for a moment, then he remembered what Kaylee said, "Do you believe you can fly?"

"It's impossible, but I'm trying."

"It's not impossible. Remember anything is possible in your dreams. Believe that you can fly. See yourself flying, soaring through the clouds and you will be able to do it."

Justin took a deep breath and then closed his eyes. He thought about flying, he thought about spreading his hands out and feeling the wind in his face. He thought about lifting from the ground and soaring through the sky and how awesome it would be.

"You're doing it!" Ryan spoke.

Justin opened his eyes to see he was hovering four feet above the ground. As soon as he looked down he fell from the air and landed on his feet.

"I can do it!" He then lifted his arms into the air, struck a Superman flying pose and pressed off the ground again. This time he shot from the grass like a rocket and into the sky past Ryan.

"Whoa!" Ryan took off after his friend.

Shooting through the clouds, higher and higher into the sky, Justin twisted, trying to direct his flight, trying to navigate. Gaining control he flew through the air, back towards Ryan. He swung around Ryan and back into the sky and yelled for joy as he swooshed past the treetops and over the land.

"Wahoo!" he screamed as he spiraled through the air, spinning like an out of control tornado. He jolted straight up and then back down again like a roller coaster. "This is great!!!" Justin swooped back down towards him and spoke, "I can't wait to show the others."

Ryan had almost forgotten there was more to do.

"That's right. Who's next - Parker?"

"Yes. Where to now?"

"There's a neighborhood just over the ridge. The pool in the backyard has the entrance to Parker's dream. He should be waiting for us there."

They flew over the landscape, Justin swooping through the trees, dodging between and around the tree trunks like a fighter pilot. Ryan watched from above with a smile. "Just up ahead."

They neared the neighborhood. Justin flew up towards Ryan and leveled out next to him. He was looking at all of the houses and backyards. Ryan pointed and tipped down toward a backyard with a pool. They landed next to the pool and looked for the light that had shone through the water.

"What now?"

"Last time it was shimmering with a weird light at the bottom."

"It's not shimmering." Justin stared at the dark pool. "What now?"

"I think I need to think about the light aisle and Parker." Ryan closed his eyes and concentrated. A moment later, Justin tapped him on the shoulder. Opening his eyes, he saw Justin staring at the pool with his mouth open. He turned to see the light shimmering and smiled. "It worked."

"Yeah it worked." Justin laughed. "How do you get through?"

"Let's just say, I hope you like to swim."

"I love to swim, but I can't open my eyes under water."

"So you won't be able to see where the porthole is?"

"Nope. You're on your own."

"Okay. I can go in alone and get Parker. You can stay here."

"Sounds good to me. I'll just stay here and work on my backstroke." Justin kicked off his shoes and peeled off his shirt. He cannon-balled into the cool pool, soaking his friend with a monstrous splash. "Come on in. The water's fine!"

Ryan wiped his face. "Yeah, I can see that." He flew straight up into the air as Justin watched, spun, and dove directly into the deep end. Like a torpedo, Ryan shot through the water and into the light, disappearing into the other side.

Chapter 12

Ryan burst through the air duct, tumbling into a puddle on the tile.

"Took you long enough." Parker sat in a lawn chair with a flashlight in his hands.

"You okay?"

"Never better. The lights are staying on because I won't let them go out." Parker grinned.

"Good for you." Ryan got to his feet and shook off the water. "You ready to go?"

"So we just crawl up into that air duct?"

"Yep."

"And then we swim up from the deep end of some swimming pool?"

"Yep."

"How will we know we made it into the pool?"

"You'll be under water."

"Oh yeah. Duh! Will I be able to breath?"

"I don't think so, but you'll just swim to the surface. It'll be fine."

"How come the water never comes into the store?" Parker asked, curious about how this whole thing worked.

"I don't know. I never thought about it." Ryan admitted as he turned.

Parker thought about it, as Ryan heaved him up to the air duct. Would the water just be like a wall? Is there a force field? Would he feel it as he merged from his dream into Ryan's world? Would there be a warning? When should he start holding his breath? How long would he have to hold his breath? Could he make it to the surface before he drowned? What if he ran out of air? Could he breathe in the water? It's a dream, would he drown? Could he die in his dream if he drowned? Maybe because it's a dream, he'd grow gills and be able to breathe under the water. Would he grow fins, like a mermaid?

Parker was deep in thought as he transferred from his dream to Ryan's. That's when all the water broke loose!

He felt the water touch his face and push past him as he swam against the pressure towards the surface. He kicked as hard as he could but felt as if he were swimming against a current. The water was rushing past him down toward the hole, the air duct they had come from. It kept flowing harder, faster. He swam and swam, kicked and kicked, worried he would run out of air, when he felt Ryan grab him by the arm and lift him into the air.

Now hovering above the water, he watched as the entire contents of the swimming pool drained through the light hole, emptying into his dream. Then he noticed Justin swimming away from the hole in the water with all his might. He was being sucked into the whirlpool.

"We've got to save him!" Parker looked up at Ryan hovering in the sky. Then he realized he was floating in the air too! He flailed in panic as Ryan swooped to catch him and drop him on the ground near the now empty pool. They watched Justin battle against the current of draining water.

"Go save him!"

"He'll be fine." Ryan said as the last of the water drained through the hole. Justin sat on the concrete floor frowning.

"Man! I was enjoying my swim." Justin groaned, then flew up out of the pool and landed next to Ryan and Parker. "Does the water drain away every time?"

"Never has before."

"What do you think happened?"

Ryan turned to Parker curiously. "What were you thinking about as you were climbing through the air duct?"

Parker thought about it then smiled shyly. "I was wondering why the water never came into the hardware store."

"Hope they have flood insurance." Justin laughed as he put his shirt and shoes back on.

Parker was confused but catching on quick enough to know that he was fine, everything was good and the plan was coming along without a hitch.

"Alright," Ryan clapped his hands together. "Let's go find Owen, Blake and Kaylee."

"Cool!" Justin shot up into the sky, "Time for school!" An odd feeling swept over him, then he added, "I never ever thought those words would come out of my mouth!"

Chapter 13

After Justin and Ryan gave Parker a flying lesson, the three had a blast racing each other through the clouds. They shot out in different directions, then about a mile out, turned, and flew back as fast as they could.

Barreling toward each other at a hundred miles per hour, their eyes widened as they shot towards each other at full speed playing chicken. Laughing, screaming, they flew closer and closer. Finally, someone had to break away; go up, go down, go left, go right. Go somewhere other than straight!

Ryan shot up. Parker turned right. Justin turned left. Unfortunately, that meant Parker and Justin turned towards one other and collided. Wham! They smacked together like a full-body high five before they tumbled to the ground like a pile of rocks.

"Parker! Justin!" Ryan yelled as he flew down to the wreck of boys on the ground. "You two okay?"

Justin realized he wasn't hurt, and glanced at Parker who jumped to his feet. "That was awesome! Let's do it again!"

Just then they heard a loud shrill, *rriiiinnnggg*. The school bell!

Parker immediately went into recess mode, "Oh man, it's class time."

Ryan, however, knew he needed to find where the sound came from. He looked all around. "That was the warning bell. It's almost time for the late bell." He hoped his words would trigger the bell to ring again. The boys kept quiet to listen.

Just then the bell rang again. The sound came from a large nest at the top of a tree.

They looked at each other curiously. Parker shrugged his shoulders, and Justin pointed to Ryan. "You heard it too, right?"

"It must have come from the nest." Ryan flew up to the nest. When he was close enough to see over the rim, a baby bird beak bigger than a football pecked at his face. He dodged it and flew higher. "Guys! You won't believe this! Come see!"

Parker and Justin soared to Ryan's side. Justin gave the nest a wide birth but Parker flew right to it unafraid. The baby birds extra large beak came dangerously close to catching his leg, but he twirled in the air as he jerked away. "What the…"

Justin was shocked by what he saw. "It's three baby birds."

Parker couldn't believe the beak that nearly snagged his leg belonged to a baby. It was the size of an alligator. He flew next to Ryan and Justin to look into the over-sized nest from a safe distance. He was appalled to see enormous baby chicks triple the size of a lion, heads, back and beaks open, waiting for food.

"Dude! They're huge!"

"Why on Earth would your dream have monster birds in it?"

"I don't know. They've never been here before." Ryan admitted.

The three boys were staring at the open-mouthed birds wondering what to do when the bell rang again. That time, the three of them realized the sound was coming from the birds.

"No way!" Justin screeched as he flew back down to the ground and landed. The other two followed.

"I know what you're thinking, and I ain't doin' it!"

"Doing what?" Parker asked clueless.

"I am NOT going to be eaten by a baby bird to get to school."

"What?" Parker coughed. "Where did you get that crazy idea?"

"You don't get it, do you?" Justin looked at Ryan to see if he was following. He still looked confused but the gears in his head were starting to turn.

"There are holes that lead into other dreams. The shimmery light hole in the deep end of a swimming pool, leads to a dream in a dark scary aisle. The hole at the base of a living tree, leads to the end of a cliff in a desert valley of death. Why not make the hole that leads to school, the mouth of a monster bird? Our mascot *is* the vulture."

"Oh man! We've got to be eaten by those birds to get to school?" Parker finally caught on.

"It looks that way." Ryan shivered. "Consumed by knowledge."

"This bites!" Justin groaned.

"Hopefully they won't." Parker smirked at his witty play on words.

Ryan took a deep breath. "We'll let's go."

"All of us?" Justin asked remembering he was able to stay behind the last time."

"There are three birds and three of us. There are also three friends in three separate dreams that need our help. I think we all have to go."

"I don't think I can." Parker stepped back as he looked back up at the daunting size of the bird nest.

"It'll be fine." Ryan spoke. "We can't be hurt in the dream. We can fly. We can heal. We can do anything we want. So if we WANT to fly into the mouths of three giant baby vultures to land in some scary scene from school, more power to us. Just remember to notice exactly where you come through so you can get back here when you have our friends."

Chapter 14

Ryan hovered above the birds and wondered which baby bird was his and whose dream he would enter. As he stared at the three hungry birds, he saw two mouths close. That was his sign. He took a deep breath and lunged forward into the bird's mouth. The bird opened his mouth wider, stretched it way out of shape, then, *shwoop.* It snapped its beak shut and swallowed Ryan, as Parker bolted behind Justin terrified at what he had just seen.

"Do you think he's okay?" Justin asked.

"He was just eaten by a monster bird! What do you think?"

"Just then the baby bird to his right opened his mouth. Justin realized that was his opening. He took a deep breath and flew into the birds mouth. *Shwoop.* When the bird closed his mouth and swallowed, Parker felt his stomach churn.

He stared long and hard at the third bird. It opened its mouth, waiting, but Parker was incapable of moving. The school bell rang from deep with its belly. He cringed at the thought. "I can't do it."

He had just decided whoever's dream it was would have to stay there when the mother bird returned to her babies.

When she saw Parker hovering there near her babies, she screeched and flexed her sharp talons. Parker turned, saw her and screeched as well. The protective bird couldn't help but go after him. He ran, or in this case, flew as fast as he could away. Through the woods, around the trunks of the trees, darting between clouds throughout the sky.

The mother vulture gained on him. Parker flew and flew, trying every move he could do to get away but she was hot on his trail. As he came around the corner of a tree, he saw he was near the baby bird nest again. The third bird's mouth was still open he noticed as he flew by, but the angry mother still chased him.

Parker didn't know what to do. He was getting tired. The only thing that would stop the momma bird, was if he flew into the baby bird's mouth. Why can't there be another way, he wondered. He knew he had to do it.

The next time he flew near the nest, he leaned right, angled low and dove down into the baby birds mouth. As he flew through the throat and down the esophagus, the throat narrowed and cooled as he felt it closing in on him. *Shwo-oo-ooop*. He was swallowed and spit right out of the blackboard in Mrs. Smith's classroom.

Tumbling onto the cold tile floor and rolling onto his back, Parker caught his breath and sat up. As he looked at the class, everyone was looking down at their desks, focusing on a quiz.

Weird! The teacher hadn't even noticed him roll in. He looked at all of the children working hard on their problems, when he saw Kaylee look up at him with a look on her face of sheer torture

"Parker! What are you doing here? You're not in my class."

"Yeah. You're not in class either. This is a dream."

"It is?" She paused thinking about it. "Of course it's a dream! I knew we hadn't studied this subject yet!" Kaylee grabbed her backpack and looked at Parker. "Okay, let's go."

"Go where?"

"Anywhere but here." Kaylee looked at the chalkboard. "You came from there, is that how we get back?"

Parker grimaced thinking about the monster birds. "I sure hope not!"

Chapter 15

Ryan oozed out of a rubber mat and laid there, a puddle in Mr. Dylan's P.E. class where he saw Blake run with a dodge ball toward one of the smaller kids. As he approached the ooze that was Ryan, he slipped and skid across the floor.

Ryan morphed back to solid form as Blake jumped up angrily to see who had tripped him. Seeing Ryan revert from ooze to human, Blake began to realize the scene wasn't real. He was starting to wrap his head around the notion when a ball thrown by the little kid rapped him on the head. *Doing!*

"You're out." Coach Dylan yelled as Blake looked on, his mouth dropped open. "That's impossible! I never lose! And especially not to a shrimp like him."

"You're dreaming," said Ryan

"What do you mean 'dreaming?' I DO always win!"

"No, you are dreaming," Ryan drew out the words slowly, "like asleep dreaming."

"I am?" Blake paused and thought for a moment. "Yeah... yeah, that makes a lot more sense!" He turned to the little kid, "You're lucky I'm dreaming or you'd never survive the rematch!"

Ryan directed Blake out of the gym door hoping he'd be able to find an alternate way out of Blake's dream world and back to his. He checked the rubber mat but didn't see any way they could get back through it.

While Ryan was pondering, Justin awoke from a desk in Mrs. James' class. Looking up, he saw Owen turned around in his chair staring at him. "I was wondering when you would get here."

"You've been waiting?"

"Ever since I lost my left molar." He held up a tooth in his hand.

"Dude! Put that back before you lose it." Justin gagged as he got up and led the two of them out of the room.

Simultaneously, the six of them walked out of the varying classrooms and into the hall. They were so excited to see each other, they ran to form a huge group hug. They emerged from the tangle of arms to see the school hall disintegrate around them. There they were, surrounded by the trees of Ryan's dream world.

"Well, that was easy."

"Easier than I expected." Parker shivered as the memory of monster bird beaks flashed in his mind.

Everyone was momentarily awe-struck but then it hit them like a wave.

"We made it!" Everyone screamed. They cheered, jumped up and down and high fived each other.

"This is so awesome!"

"Totally!"

"We're free!"

"We can do whatever we want!"

"Yeah!"

"Go anywhere we want!"

"No rules!"

"No curfew!"

"No bedtime!"

"No vegetables at dinner!"

"We are the coolest kids in the world!"

"In the universe!"

"Yeah!"

They all stared at each other, smiling brightly, excited... they continued to stare, eyes shifting, right and left. They looked at each other, carefully, curiously. Their faces went from excitement to confusion.

"Uh... what do we want to do?"

"I don't know. What do you want to do?"

"Any ideas?"

"Uh..."

They continued to stand there. Some shifted their feet on the ground, others wrung their hands together.

"Uh..."

Deep in thought, Parker tried to come up with something to do. He pressed the bridge of his glasses back up his nose. The act of repositioning his glasses had become so routine; he'd never even given it much thought, until now. It was annoying. This was the dream world. He shouldn't have to wear glasses!

Just then Parker declared boldly, "Well I'm not wearing glasses here!" He took off his glasses and threw them to the ground. He stomped on them then looked up at the shocked faces of the others. He saw Kaylee's freckles dotting her face. He read the logo on Justin's black shirt. He scrunched his eyes then widened them. "Guys! I've got perfect vision!"

Everyone looked at him curiously.

"Well," said Kaylee, ever the wise one, "of course you do. If you want it, you can have it. We are in the dream world."

Just then Blake declared, "I want a Mohawk! A purple and blue striped Mohawk on my head!" Blake's hair moved, twisted, grew and discolored on its own. Within a few seconds, his multi-colored hair pointed straight out from his skull.

"Me too, with spikes," Ryan added, trying to top his friend. Just then, his hair sprouted a spiky dark blue hair style that made him look like a punk rocker. "And punk rock makeup!" Multiple lightning bolts flashed on his face and dark coloring outlined his eyes. "Now I need a black leather jacket." Black leather seemed to grow down his arms and back. "With spikes and chains!" Large metal spikes emerged from his shoulders, and chains hung from around his neck.

It was clear, he looked cooler than Blake, so Blake altered his image to that of a ninja complete with sword. *Swish, swish.* He sliced through the air performing perfect ninja moves.

A green mask materialized around Owen's eyes and a green cape draped down his back from his neck. With tights and muscles to match, Owen looked like a green and yellow superhero and he began flexing his mighty biceps to show off.

Kaylee, holding her mouth shut while she blew on her thumb, grew her hair out in long perfect spirals. A bejeweled gold crown appeared on her head with matching necklace and earrings that completed her princess look. She was so elegant and grand the boys couldn't help but stare.

Justin then morphed into a hip hop star. He strummed a guitar, and it was so loud it rattled the land. Everyone else changed into rock stars and began playing instruments along with him.

Ryan beat the drums in a cool solo. Owen played the saxophone and Parker fiddled a tune that smoked the strings. Kaylee changed into a lead singer and somehow, even though everyone was playing their own thing, their jam session sounded amazing.

The green hill they had been standing on transformed into a stage complete with a laser light show and flame throwing effects. A screaming crowd of fans appeared before them, and they were just going wild. The six of them jammed for a whole session, playing blaring rock music until they finally stopped for a break.

Tall cool glasses of lemonade appeared in their hands. Sitting on the stage relaxing, wondering what to do next, the platform dissolved back into the ground and they found themselves sitting on the grass.

Parker began picking at blades of grass as Blake began poking at an anthill. Kaylee though, decided to try some magic. She touched a wildflower with the tip of her finger. *Poof,* it broke apart into a dozen pieces. Each piece produced a butterfly and all of the butterflies flew away in a vibrant swirl of color. Loving how beautiful the sight was, she touched another flower, then another. *Poof. Poof.* Each morphed into a dozen butterflies of varying colors and flew across the grass past the boys who were watching.

Taking the idea a step further, Blake touched a long blade of grass and morphed it into a green grass snake that slithered through his fingers. Kaylee scooted away from him.

Ryan then began touching things and watched them disappear. He'd touch a flower and it'd disappear. He touched a tree and watched it shoot down to the ground and disappear. "Where did it go?"

Owen decided to bring his dog Smurphy to the dream world. He closed his eyes, thought real hard of his bestest fur friend, and then, *arf,* his sweet red-haired golden retriever appeared in front of him, all excited. Smurphy's tail wagged, his tongue dangled out of his smiling mouth and he was so ready to play, his fur was standing on end.

Ryan was touching everything he could find to see if it would disappear, a log a rock, a dog...

"Smurphy!" Owen screamed as his best friend disappeared leaving just a few strands of red fur behind. "What did you do?" Owen growled at Ryan.

"I don' know!"

"Where's my dog?"

The other kids ran up as Owen grew angrier. "If something bad happened to my dog I swear!"

"Did you hear that?" Kaylee spoke quick. Everyone shushed.

Arf, arf.

"Smurphy?" Owen called. "Smurphy boy, where are you?"

Arf, arf.

Owen followed the sound to the ground, getting closer and closer until he saw a microscopic dog about the size of a beetle jumping from the ground trying to get his master's attention.

"Smurphy! What are you doing down there?" His dog was so small and so far away it broke his heart. He knew he had to do something. He looked at Ryan who was staring at the tiny dog with his mouth dropped open. Thinking quickly, he grabbed Ryan's hand and touched his finger to his head. Owen shrank to the size of Smurphy so he could be with his dog.

"Cool!" said Parker, "Do me!" Ryan touched him, and he shrank down. Everyone else followed. Smiling, yet shrugging his shoulders, Ryan touched his head and also shot down to microscopic size.

Ryan's world looked completely different from this level. Each blade of grass was the size of a tall tree. Each pebble was the size of a car. They climbed grass like trees, hopped over drops of water the size of ponds and rode ants the size of horses. The kids had a blast until Blake's green grass snake slithered up. The scaly giant towered over them at least five stories tall and stared at them like they were snacks.

"Ahhhh!" Kaylee screamed. The boys though, took action. They took defender stances with their fists on their hips and suddenly shot back up to proper size. The snake, now harmless, slithered away in fear.

Kaylee returned to proper size with Smurphy, grateful the snake was gone.

Owen ran to Smurphy and gave him a big hug. "Hi boy!" He smiled rubbing Smurphy's floppy ears. Owen then decided the dream world might be too dangerous for his furry friend and so, with a little sadness, he sent Smurphy home.

"Bye little buddy! I'll see you soon."

Chapter 16

"Cheerio" came a voice with a thick British accent. "Where did that dog go?" The voice was coming from within the trees. The kids looked up wondering who was there when a blue bird flew down and landed on a log next to them. "Cat got your tongue?"

"You can talk?" Parker asked, his mouth dropping open as he stared at the bird.

Seeing this, Ryan decided he should bring his pet parrot into the dream world. He'd been trying to teach it the phrase "Polly want a cracker?" for a very long time, unsuccessfully. He concentrated on the smooth yellow feathers of his pet, and *shwoop!* As the bird flew in and landed on his shoulder, Ryan pointed at the blue bird, can you talk like him?" The parrot listened for a few moments then shook his head no. "Why not?" Ryan asked completely disappointed.

"Because, me friend," he began with an Irish accent, "I'm from the land of leprechauns." Just then two leprechauns popped out of rainbows and scurried across the land carrying a big black pot of gold. Every step they took, large shamrocks shot up from the ground and within a few seconds the entire hillside was covered in clovers.

Parker picked one of the clovers and looked at it. "It's a four leaf clover! I'm going to have good luck!"

He held the clover up for the others to see as the blue bird flew off and dropped a gooey white gift on his hand.

"Eww! Bird poop!"

When shaking his hand didn't help, he wiped the poo on Owen's back when he wasn't paying attention.

Ryan's parrot stretched his wings and flew toward Parker. As he approached, he got bigger and bigger. When he landed on the ground next to Parker he was the size of a dragon.

"Awesome! Let's go flying." Owen said, as he pivoted in place, trying to figure out what Parker put on his back. All six kids climbed onto the back of the oversized bird. They held on tight as he took off toward the sky, flying faster than they ever dreamed.

"Woohoo!" Justin held his arms up like he would in a roller coaster ride. At that moment, the parrot made a sharp turn. Justin and Blake both fell off the bird and were barreling towards the ground at full speed. Justin's woohoo changed to "Waahhh!"

Luckily Blake dreamed up a large black cat leaping to catch them. As a black panther the size of a double-decker bus caught the two kids on his back, Blake took hold of the reins and the trio began to chase the bird.

The panther extended its claws and swatted at the bird. In retaliation, the giant parrot dive-bombed the cat, flinging the kids to the ground. They rolled to safety just before being trampled by the Godzilla meets King Kong fight going on in front of them.

Suddenly, Mothra (one of the villains from the Godzilla movies), a fleet of aliens and four different types of dinosaurs stomped in to the dream world creating mini earthquakes with each step they took. Any creature that came into their minds appeared before them and joined the fight.

"Alright, who thought about the Stay Puffed Marshmallow Man from the Ghostbusters movie?"

Owen smirked as the kids scrambled for safety behind trees or rocks. All found cover but one – Kaylee. The boys yelled at her over squawks and hisses. "C'mon!" "Kaylee you're gonna get stomped on!" "Yeah, don't try to be a hero!"

But Kaylee had decided THAT was exactly what she was going to do. She knew the only way to regain control of their world was to become the superheroes it so desperately needed. She became the Straw berry Wind Sprite, a flying super hero, wearing red and pink tights. She boldly burst into the sky, held her hands out and shot wind from her palms. Miraculously, monster after monster were knocked off their feet.

Kaylee looked around to find that Blake, Ryan and Owen had followed suit. Ryan, the Blue Blaze flew into the realm shooting lasers from his eyes. Owen, the Green Power Fighter, picked up a large tree and swung it like a baseball bat at the villains. Then Blake, the Black Wolf scratched and froze the giant monsters. When the area had been saved Justin and Parker came out from hiding to applaud their super-friends.

Moments later, the superheroes found themselves riding on a highly decorated parade float going down a busy street with adoring fans screaming and shouting their names. Girls swooned while others shouted, "Our heroes!"

Fireworks shot into the air. Like a switch that was flipped, the blue sky immediately turned to night so the firework bursts could radiate the darkness with their vibrant colors.

When the parade was over, the six children lay on the ground and looked up at the stars, relaxing. "Is it really night time already?" Owen asked, starting to yawn like the dark was a visual cue for him to be tired.

"No way!" Blake jumped up, "I am not going to let it be night yet. We are having way too much fun!"

Just then, the moon became the sun and the sky popped from black to blue. Birds in the trees began singing again.

"I'm hungry." Parker exclaimed as he sat up and rubbed his belly.

"Me too." Ryan smiled as he made a dining table pop up from the ground followed by chairs that scooped up all of the kids and walked four-legged to the table. "And I want cake!" Immediately a three tiered cake, fully decorated and dripping with chocolate appeared before him.

"I want pie!" Parker smiled as a large round pie appeared on a plate with six different flavors and designs in the one pie. "Look, I've got peach, cherry, key lime, apple, pumpkin and chocolate pie pieces!" Kaylee leaned over to admire the intricately designed yet perfectly formed six individual and unique slices of pie.

"I want pizza!" Blake spoke, "Twelve meats with extra cheese and pineapples."

"What twelve meats are there?" Kaylee asked.

"Ham, sausage ground beef, bacon, pepperoni, bologna, Canadian bacon, hot dogs, chicken, pork chops, meatballs and steak." Blake spoke most assuredly.

"Yeah." Justin grabbed a slice so weighed down with toppings he had to use three hands to hold it.

Owen eyed Justin's third hand and followed it to his left side where even his shirt had an additional sleeve. Owen poked at the third arm curiously, but Justin groaned, "Dude, you almost made me drop my pizza!"

Kaylee ate a large fruit salad, but when her bowl was empty, she filled it with ice cream. Vanilla with raspberry, cinnamon, blueberries and chocolate with sprinkles.

"A banana split!" One of the kids exclaimed as he dropped his pizza to the table and made a quadruple sundae appear before him with whipped cream and cherries.

"I want 33 flavors with all of the toppings in a waffle cone!" Parker laughed as the largest most colorful waffle boat of ice cream appeared on the table in front of him.

As he began eating, he looked up at everyone else's concoctions. It was like Wonka's chocolate factory mixed with the witch's gingerbread house and the mega candy store at the mall all rolled into one!

Chapter 17

Kaylee realized she was thirsty and a glass of water appeared in her hand. She took a slow sip. Glancing over at Blake, she noticed him raise an inquisitive eyebrow. "What?"

"Plain water?"

"Yeah?"

"How about some flavored ice?" A grape, cherry and lemon ice cube appeared in her glass. The tri-colored cubes clinked and shimmered in the mid day sun. Parker decided he was hot and wanted a large grape ice cube to suck on, but Owen took it a step farther. He squinted his eyes in concentration, and a giant grape glacier grew out of the ground. The table and chairs flattened, and the kids found themselves standing on an oversized ice rink in the sky. Each wore various colored ice skates.

"I love to ice skate." Ryan took off down the rink. A trail of orange liquid flowed out from behind his orange skates.

Blake skated leaving a dark purplish-black trail behind his black skates. He skidded to a stop at the trail of orange and bent down to taste it. "Cool! It tastes like orange kool-aid."

"What?! The streaks are flavored?" Kaylee asked as she skated around leaving reddish-pink streaks. She tasted the pink, then Blake's black. "Mine is strawberry, and his is blackberry."

Justin's skates were green with the flavor of lime. Parker wore yellow and his flavor was pineapple. Owen wore blue so, of course, his was raspberry (because that makes sense). The six of them twirled and skated on the ice, then purposely fell and slid across it like a slip-and-slide. They rode with their mouths open to catch the icy flavors.

Kaylee grabbed Ryan's hand, then had him grab Parker, then had Parker grab Justin, Owen then Blake. She put them in order - red, orange, yellow, green, blue and purple. The six of them made a rainbow as they skated in order leaving flowing wet trails of fruit flavored streams behind them.

A gust of wind then picked up the colors and lifted them into the air, creating a rainbow. Kaylee released the boys hands and skated towards the rainbow. She lifted her legs higher and was able to skate onto her rainbow. She found she could control the colorful arch with her movements. It led her higher and higher, so much so that she disappeared from sight.

Parker skated to the edge of the glacier where it was quickly melting in the sun, creating a cascading waterfall. He shed his skates and clothes for swim trunks and dove into the waterfall allowing the waters to create a waterslide that defied gravity. The waters would fall straight down then with the whimsy of a twisty straw, the water shot up and created angles and curves like a roller coaster. He imagined a large inner tube to sit on and gave himself the ride of his life. A waterslide that would never end – unless he wanted it to.

Blake and Justin created bumper race cars to do donuts and drift across the ice. They raced each other, creating a track and throwing up obstacles for each other.

Watching everyone else having fun, Owen decided it was time for some fun of his own - practical jokes. He became ghost-like and hid behind a tree. He jumped out, appearing in front of the boys' cars making them swerve to miss him, skid out of control and crash. As the boys got out of their cars, angry at Owen, Owen turned ghost-like again and sunk down into the glacier.

Once Owen turned back into himself and stood in the center of the glacier, he decided it needed something more. He melted the center of the glacier, creating an underwater world where he turned into a merman with gills and swam under the sea. He created sea creatures and fish and a whole underwater city where he was the king who controlled the tides.

Blake and Justin, unable or unwilling to follow Owen into the center of the glacier, turned back to their wrecked ice bumper cars and recreated them into flying air ships. Once hovering in the sky, they shot disintegrating lasers at the glacier leaving Owen and his underwater world flopping around like fish on dry land.

"Hey, why did you do that?" He asked as Blake and Justin laughed at him from their spaceships.

"One practical joke deserves another."

Chapter 18

After Owen turned his fins and gills back into normal human legs, Justin transported Owen to his flying ship using a light beam then keyed in the wide open sky into the ships navigation module. Their jet engines were revving to fly off to a new adventure when Parker approached riding his wacky waterslide.

"Hey guys, whatcha doin?"

"We're about to explore the sky but your waterslide looks cool!"

"Well then join me."

Parker engineered his inner tube into a flying ship like theirs and the three connected like a train. Ready for an out-of-this-world ride, parker made the waterslide as crazy as he could imagine and they boys rode it with glee.

"Guys I'm gonna hurl!" Owen groaned holding his stomach with one hand and covering his mouth with the other.

"Dude! You look like that picture they took on that roller coaster ride at Six Flags last summer.

"Roller Coaster! Great idea!" Parker laughed pumping the sky with his fist as the water hardened into steel tracks. Their ships became more aerodynamic as they soared along the rails. They went up, down and spiraled into loopty-loops on the wildest most outrageous high-speed coaster they could possibly imagine.

They rode straight up into the sky a million miles, then slowly came over the top of the hill only to go straight down at a zillion miles per hour directly into the ground, tunneling their way to the center of the Earth.

"Dude, it's getting hot." Owen croaked as they neared Earth's core. Blake turned the track upwards and they shot up through the middle of a volcano until they erupted out the other side like a rocket on fire.

"We're going to explode!" Owen screamed with terror as he took a deep breath and closed his eyes.

"Not if we don't let it," yelled Blake. "Everybody think spaceships!"

Their red hot metal roller coaster transformed into three cool sleek space ship rockets.

"Now lets go look for some aliens!" yelled Parker.

As they shot around the dark side of the moon they came across a shimmering UFO with lights spinning around the center like a disco ball. The sudden jolt of red laser lights flickering in the dark blackness of space caught Blake completely off guard. Terrified the aliens were shooting at them, Blake initiated attack pattern alpha, opening fire on the space aliens who instantly started to fly away.

"We've got them on the run boys!" Blake yelled through his intercom to Owen and Parker who followed in hot pursuit. The three shot and chased the aliens throughout star clusters and galaxies starting what could have been an intergalactic war.

"They are going to get away!" Parker yelled as Justin shot left around a meteor to cut them off.

"Not if I can help it!"

The four boys chased the aliens around planets, stars and meteors, shooting orange and green lasers. When the orange lasers, struck the aliens' shields, they turned various shades of green and purple and bounced back at the boys, forcing them to dodge their own shots.

The aliens sensed they were out-numbered though and could see that their shields were weakening. They knew they didn't stand a chance against these crazy human assassins.

Suddenly, a rainbow appeared in the midst of the black sky of space directly before them.

The aliens who'd never seen a rainbow were terrified and flew directly through it. The boys ships swerved to miss and skidded to a stop in front of it.

The boys stared open mouthed as Kaylee in full space gear, rode her flying rainbow motorcycle to the middle of the boys' alien battle.

Skidding to a stop before them, she yelled, "What are you guys doing?"

"Fighting the aliens."

"Why? What did they do to you?"

"They're aliens!" Blake scoffed as if that were enough of an excuse. "This is our dream world. We're going to defend it!"

Just then, the alien's ship rounded the edge of the rainbow and peeked out from behind Kaylee's motorcycle. They began speaking and clacking inaudible sounds, unsuccessfully attempting to communicate.

"What are they trying to say?" Parker asked. Blake and Owen shook their heads and shrugged their shoulders, but Justin noticed Kaylee nod her head.

"Yeah, I know they can be a bunch of hot heads. I'll tell them." She turned to the boys.

"Tell us what?"

"You can understand them?" the guys asked.

"Of course, I can understand them. You guys aren't wearing your universal translators are you?" She pulled out four sets of purple ear buds and transported them into each of the boys' hands. Plugging the translators into their ears, they immediately understood what the aliens were saying.

"Shooting at us like space cowboys..."

"Crazy kids, don't even realize we have their King."

"Our King? We don't have a king."

"Of course, you have a king. He is called President Pharaoh Ryan the First, King of Dreamstonia."

The boys and Kaylee stared at each other curiously. Kaylee then realized. "Where is Ryan?"

"Abducted by the aliens." Ryan called out as he stuck his head out the window of the alien's spacecraft. "Good thing you guys didn't shoot us down!"

"Dude! When did that happen?"

"Right about the time the wind began swirling around me and my orange skates. It created a tornado that lifted me into space attracting the attention of Fred and Bob here."

"Fred and Bob?" Everyone repeated in unison, nearly laughing at the ridiculous names for these aliens.

"Yeah, I call them Fred and Bob because their real names are way too hard for me to say."

Everyone stared at the greenish-grey aliens with large black eyes and green tentacles reaching out of their heads. The dreamers smiled as Fred and Bob waved hi.

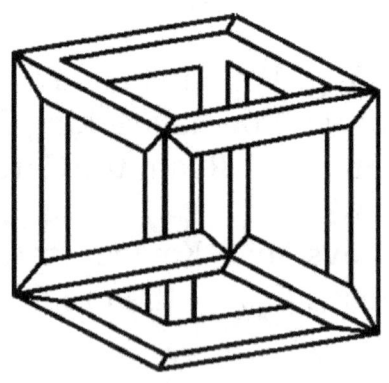

Chapter 19

That evening, the kids followed the aliens back to their world and boy was it different. There were grey trees, black grass, and an olive green sky with yellow streaks. This was hardly a colorful world, but worked well to blend the aliens' grayish-green skin and large black eyes into the scenery like camouflage.

There were tall buildings that twisted upward, spiraling into the air like unicorn horns. From the top, there were long, pointy spires that pointed outwards like the Statue of Liberty's crown. What looked like floating homes in round bubbles were connected to the ground by clear tubes with elevators. There were two-headed, dragon-looking creatures flying in the sky. They breathed grayish-green smoke that encompassed their scaly grey bodies and wings so they hid in the sky inside their own self-made clouds.

The kids gushed with awe and wonder as they took in the alien planet.

"Dude, did you see that?" Blake gawked at a three-headed green bird that flew into a cloud.

"Yeah, but did you see those?" Justin pointed up to the sky at three square shaped space craft coming in for a landing.

"I can't seem to take my eyes off of that!" Owen pointed at a nearby building that seemed like an optical illusion the way it connected to each section.

"Come children, it is time to be dinner." Fred smiled unaware of his language error.

Whipping their heads around, the kids were relieved when Bob smacked Fred on the arms and corrected his sentence.

"Not *be* dinner, *see* dinner."

"See dinner? Isn't it for dinner?"

"Not see for dinner but come for dinner."

"Come? Should be do?"

"Do dinner works but maybe it should be eat?"

Fred smiled and turned to the confused children. "Come children, it is time to be eaten for dinner."

Bob dropped his head into his hand in defeat as Kaylee spoke brightly.

"Yes, guys lets join Fred and Bob for dinner."

Fred nodded his head happily and led the way as the boys exchanged suspicious glances at each other.

They followed their hosts to a large room with a huge metal table that stretched twenty feet long. They sat down and were brought plate after plate of alien delicacies: pineapple shaped squid with curly tentacles that swayed in a spicy brown sauce and green asparagus looking worms with talons and eyes that popped out of their head.

Owen thought he might gag at the mere sight of his dinner, but when he watched Fred and Bob dig in he was certain he was going to throw up.

Justin and Blake listened in horror as a green asparagus worm screamed as it was swallowed by Bob. But Ryan couldn't wait to try. He grabbed one in each hand. Opening his mouth to taste the one in his left hand, the worm began screaming. He looked at it, and decided to try the one on the right instead. As soon as he turned to the other, it too started screaming. It was almost too loud to stand so Ryan brought them both up to his mouth and bit their heads off simultaneously. The silence was instant and after Ryan swallowed, he exclaimed. "These worm-things are awesome! They taste just like corn dogs!"

Without a second thought, the others dug in excited to try their screaming corndogs.

Owen still felt hesitant about the worms, so he took a spoonful of the light grey mashed potato looking glop and tapped it onto his plate. He sniffed – yuck! Wet gym socks! Dropping his spoon, he noticed a red gelatin material that looked like jello. It smelled safe enough, so he carefully took a microscopic bite. It moved and expanded in his mouth until his cheeks were completely expanded and he finally spit it back out onto his plate.

"What the heck was that?"

Fred looked at him. "Tsk, tsk, tsk. Red Swell, expands with liquid until swallowed. Must swallow quickly."

"Now you tell me."

Owen, gagged with every moving tentacle, expanding goo and scream the food made, but the rest of the kids seemed to enjoy the cuisine quite a bit.

When they were done with their dinner, they all sat around and watched the alien's pet Drupa dance and fly around the room. The seven-legged Drupa was very much like a dog except it has scales instead of fur and tentacles instead of ears – and of course, it flew.

That evening the kids rested on floating mats surrounded by trellises of grayish-green ivy and looked up at the stars that were much closer than they had ever seen before. In fact, Ryan was certain a couple of stars winked at him.

The next morning the kids woke up back in Ryan's original dream world. "How did we get back here? Where are the aliens?"

"I don't know. Maybe we were returned by Fred and Bob?"

"So they un-abducted us?"

"Works for me."

"So what should we do today?"

"Let's go swimming." Kaylee suggested. Her plan seemed simple enough but as the land began to ooze and sway, the boys realized she wasn't thinking about a simple backyard swimming pool.

The world transformed into ocean, and before they knew it, the boys were floating in sapphire blue waters.

"Cool!"

Parker had his back turned to Justin when a large wave rushed over his head and pushed him under. He fought to get to the surface as the others bounced up to ride over it.

"Not cool, guys." Parker gasped for breath.

Ryan, Justin, Blake and Owen imagined they were surfers and colorful surfboards appeared under their bodies.

"I can't surf!" Parker spoke as a surfboard appeared under him as well.

"What do you mean? We're in the dream world – you can do anything!"

"Here it comes!" Ryan announced as a large wave came barreling towards them. "Hang ten!"

Kaylee watched the five take off surfing the tube when she willed her legs into fins and dove down into the depths of the ocean as a mermaid.

About an hour later, they boys were sprawled out on the beach soaking up some sun and resting when Kaylee called to them from a nearby buoy.

"Ready for another adventure?"

"What are you doing out there?" Parker called to her, shielding his eyes from the mid day sun.

"Oh, just holding a treasure map wondering if anyone is interested in a hunt."

"Treasure hunt!" The boys chimed gleefully, leaping to their feet and giving each other high fives. "Where is it?"

"Under water – through a labyrinth of rocky caves."

"How will we get to it?"

"Well, I've got gills." Kaylee lifted her mermaid tail from the waters and splashed it down again.

Owen was all for it. He transformed himself back into a merman and dove into the waters. When he emerged near Kaylee, he looked back to the beach to see the other guys just standing there.

"What are you waiting for?"

"Dude – mermaids are dorky."

"Are not." Owen scolded.

"Then be something else." Kaylee suggested. "Turn yourselves into another ocean creature."

Justin liked that idea. He leapt to the waters becoming a dolphin. When he came up, all Parker and Blake could hear was the high-pitched squeaking and clicking of dolphin sounds.

"What is he saying?"

"Where are your universal translators?" Kaylee asked.

"Oh right!" They imagined their ear buds in their hands and placed them back in their ears. Now they could hear Justin.

"Come on guys! Change into something."

Parker, not wanting to be a woosy dolphin became a large killer whale. It took him a few minutes to wriggle out to the deeper waters, but he made it. Ryan became an octopus.

"Not wanting to be outdone though, Blake shape shifted into a shark. He swam circles around Owen – that dark black shark fin circled closer and closer to him. It was an eerie, I'm-gonna-get-eaten feeling, until Kaylee smacked the water.

"Stop that!"

Blake lifted his head from the water and smiled with his enormously large mouth of razor sharp teeth. "Sorry – I don't know what came over me."

Chapter 20

"Let's go!" Kaylee called before diving back into the waters and leading the way. The boys; merman, dolphin, octopus, shark and enormous killer whale followed as she led them deeper, deeper into the dark depths of the ocean.

As it grew darker, their eyes grew accustomed and pulled light from various places to illuminate their path. Kaylee pointed to a rocky under water tunnel and dove down even further until they all stopped at the entrance, and glanced in.

"What now?"

Kaylee pulled out the treasure map and showed them. Owen followed the dotted line with his finger until he got to the X.

"Okay, it doesn't actually show the labyrinth of caves but each turn the line takes is probably very important. We'll have to follow this precisely or we'll get lost for sure."

"Okay though – one question." Parker interrupted. "How am I supposed to fit in there?" He gestured to the cave entrance that was much, much smaller than him.

The team looked at the enormous killer whale and Kaylee coughed back a giggle.

"What?"

"You may need to shrink yourself down."

Parker thought hard about his situation and shrunk his giant whale body to about the size of the others - shark, dolphin, octopus and mer-folk. "Better?"

Blake laughed loudly. "You look like a baby whale!"

"Awe, but he's so cute!" Kaylee cooed as she tickled under his chin.

"Stop it!" Parker brushed her hand away with his fin. "It's just for the hunt."

"Sure." Blake laughed again.

The six then swam into the labyrinth of caves and through each tunnel following the map. Many times they came upon multiple openings and had to determine which way to go but the map was incredibly detailed. Just shy of the big red X, they came to grand cave room the size of a football field. There were so many cave openings lining its walls, so many choices; there was no way they could decide.

"What do we do now?"

Kaylee looked at the map, then at the dozens of holes - some to the left, some to the right, some above her, some below her.

"We'll each take a cave and see where it goes." Justin suggested.

"Great, but what about the other twenty caves?" Blake groaned.

Parker shrugged his proverbial shoulders.

"What was that? A hick-up?" Owen asked.

"I shrugged my shoulders."

"You don't have any shoulders."

Just then Parker imagined what a dolphin with shoulders would look like and bony, awkward projections emerged from his smooth rubbery dolphin skin. The shoulders pulled his fins out from his side to become more like arms and he then flexed his non-muscular fin biceps, attempting to look cool.

"Gross!" Justin nearly gagged. "What on earth did you do to yourself?"

"I gave myself shoulders."

"That is just plain wrong!"

Ryan and Owen had gone to scout the first two tunnels and found that about fifty feet in, they were blocked off.

"We just need to find the one tunnel that actually goes through." Ryan spoke definitively.

"What makes you think there is just one?"

"Let's find out."

Ryan went in a hole to the left and came out of a hole on the right. Kaylee went up into one on the ceiling and came out of one on the floor. Of course by the time they all met back in the center, they had lost track of which way was up and which holes they had tried.

They decided they had to try again this time marking the holes. It was like an optical illusion watching them go up and come down, swim left and flow right. It reminded Kaylee of that image by artist M. C. Escher of the stairs that went in all sorts of directions.

Finally, they narrowed the numerous cave openings down to two. "It's one of those." Parker said definitively. "Should we split up?"

"Probably not." Kaylee looked at both openings. "We'll take this one." She pointed to the one on the right.

The others followed her in, except Parker – the dolphin with shoulders. Parker already felt different enough being the dolphin with shoulders. *I'm not going to follow the pack. I do my own thing.* He swam into the cave on the left, wondering silently where it was going to lead.

As the group emerged from the other side of the cave, they saw it. A sparkling pile of gold, jewels and pearls, piled around a large wooden treasure chest that was so full the lid couldn't close.

"We found it!" Blake speedily swam to it, followed by the others.

As they neared, they became disoriented. Something was gathering them together, sweeping them into a collected heap. They squirmed and wriggled only to find themselves being pulled up out of the waters by a large net.

The mass of fish and bodies weighed the net down as they emerged from the water. They swung through the air before, hovering over the deck of a large wooden ship. The hooks holding the net released, dropping the load in the middle of two dozen pirates.

"What's going on?" Kaylee asked, attracting the pirate's attention to her.

"A mermaid!" one of the pirates exclaimed.

"Leave her alone." Owen growled, flailing on the pile of slimy fish.

"A mermaid... boy?" Another pirate spoke with hesitation.

"That's merman." Owen corrected.

"Don't talk to the pirates." Parker recalled his mother's don't talk to strangers speech.

"Look guys, a baby killer whale." Another pirate spoke.

"He's adorable." others laughed.

"I'm not a baby! I'm just smaller than regular."

"And it talks!" Another pirate spoke with fear.

A few pirates backed away. "It's a demon whale."

"We can take 'em." Blake the shark suggested, but that backfired.

In a flash, the pirates pulled out their swords, ready to fight.

"Now what?" Kaylee sat back worried.

Just then, a brilliant white laser beam blasted a hole in the deck of the pirate ship. The pirates cowered and looked up at the source of the blast.

Hovering above their heads was a large red metal man with a bright round light on his chest. He shot another beam at the mast of the pirate ship and as the pole and crow's nest fell towards the deck, the pirates all leapt from the ship into the water, screaming in fear.

The metal man took off his helmet as he landed on the deck.

"Parker?"

"Why are you dressed like Ironman?"

"Why are you wearing an eye patch?"

He put his hands on his hips and puffed out his chest, "You can call me – the Iron Pirate!"

Everyone laughed as they and their surroundings transformed back to Ryan's original dream world.

Image Courtesy of M. C. Escher

Image Courtesy of M. C. Escher

Chapter 21

The next morning, after the group finished breakfast, they discussed what they were going to do next.

"All I know is, today we have got to figure out how to top ourselves! What should we do?"

With a desire to do bigger and better things, more than they did yesterday or the day before, they had to get creative. They decided to face their challenge by creating a time machine. It was the shape of the Death Star, a large round ball, and they used it to roll through time in any direction they wanted.

Once they decided where to go – or when to go - they'd wind up the pitch and then roll themselves down the star streaked sky like a bowling ball and shoot to whatever time they wanted.

Their first stop? Egypt.

There in the sand dunes, they watched Fred and Bob's alien ancestors blast off, leaving the Egyptians with plans for building their first pyramid.

Next stop - the future. They weren't exactly sure which year they landed in - but there was technology everywhere and everyone seemed to be playing virtual games as their real lives.

"Whatcha doin?" Blake asked a kid wearing virtual goggles and ear buds. He tapped on the kids arm. Slowly, reluctantly, the kid removed his goggles.

His eyes were almost completely white and he squinted in the sun.

"Watcha doin?" Blake asked again.

"Why aren't you wearing your Realty Specs?" The boy asked, shielding his eyes from the light.

"Reality Specs?" Kaylee cut in.

The future kid looked at all six of the dreamers before him, his face stunned and appalled. "You're not connected to anything? No Specs, no Ear Set. How are you even surviving without any tech?"

"What do you mean? The world is beautiful and clean. Take a look."

The future kid looked around and was shocked. "This is amazing. It looks just like it does in my Realty Specs. Freaky."

"Hold up," Justin interrupted. "You live your entire life wearing virtual reality gear without ever looking out at the real world?"

The kid looked at him quizzically.

"What do you do all day?"

"Live the life. We can do anything we want to. If I want to climb the side of a building I just do it."

"You can defy gravity?"

"You can do anything. Here, watch." The kid said putting his Reality Specs back on. The dreamers watched the kid approach a building, look up, and then lift his leg like he was about to walk up the side. He staggered a bit, leaning backwards.

"See?" He spoke as he turned back to the kids.

The kids glanced at each other. The boy hadn't climbed anywhere.

"With Reality Specs," he continued, "you can defy gravity. I can even fly. Wanna see?"

"Sure." Said Owen, wanting to see what the kid did to make himself *think* he was flying.

The kid gave them a thumbs up, then lifted his hands into the air and pressed off with his feet. He walked around, swerving his arms in large curves as if he were flying in the air. Then he looked straight ahead (which to him was down) and waved at the kids. "Go get your Reality Specs. Life's no fun if you can't fly." Then he walked away, arms extended flying through his Virtual World.

"How sad is that?" Kaylee spoke, thinking about how gullible future kids were.

"Sad?" Owen exclaimed, "I want a pair of Reality Specs!"

"Dude," Blake laughed, "Did you not see that he wasn't *really* flying? He only *thought* he was flying."

"Yeah but, I can't even THINK I'm flying in our real world."

"Whatever." Blake laughed and looked back at the 'flying' kid who must have thought he was miles away by now but had only traveled about twenty yards. "That's so sad."

Chapter 22

"When to next?" Owen asked thinking about how cool a prehistoric jungle would be. Before they knew it the time machine had rolled them into the land of dinosaurs.

They all leapt out of the large ball and gazed at the world before them.

"WOW!!!" Owen exclaimed cheerfully.

"I'm going to find some herbivores." Kaylee declared.

"I'm with Kaylee." Parker added.

"Well I'm gonna find me some carnivores!" Blake grinned ready for a rumble. Justin decided that would be fun so he stepped near Blake.

"That leaves you with me." Ryan said to Owen.

"Why's that?"

"We should go in pairs."

"Safety in numbers." Kaylee added matter-of-factly.

"She's right." Justin added.

"But what about Blake and Justin?" Owen questioned. "They're going hunting for carnivores. Anyone see the movie Jurassic Park?"

"Dude," Blake laughed, "That's a movie. This is the dream world. We can do anything we want here."

"Even kick some T-Rex butt!" Justin added, punching his fist in the air.

Kaylee, was eager to get started on her own quest. She headed toward the jungle with Parker a few steps behind.

Immediately immersed in massive green palm leaves, curled feather-like ferns and towering trunks of prehistoric trees; the two walked on admiring their surroundings.

The noises of the jungle sounded like modern day jungle sounds, but they were abstract as well. Animals that would be considered screeching monkeys sounded like over-sized gorillas. A parrots' call sounded more like clanging cymbals. And the constant background sound of chirping crickets sounded more like the rumblings of a very hungry tummy.

The noises were enough to give Parker the willies but the vegetation, swaying in the breeze made him feel as if the branches were reaching out for him. Every vine he brushed against made him quiver, and when a new sound entered his ears, he'd let loose a muffled scream.

"Look here." Kaylee knelt down near a hollowed out tree trunk. "I saw eyes shining in there."

"So you decided to kneel down next to it like a sacrifice?"

"Herbivores, Parker. It will most likely be a plant eater and will mean us no harm."

"Most likely... it could be one of those that eat both plant and meat."

"An omnivore? No, not likely." Kaylee strummed her fingers on the bottom of the trunk, enticing the small critter out of its hole. Parker watched from afar as a small, somewhat furry opossum-looking creature stuck its head out of its hole.

"I think this is a Maotherium."

"A Mayo-what?"

"Maotherium, just recently found in Asia and supposedly nocturnal. I read an article about it just last week. Are you tired little guy?"

"I think he's looking to see where his enormous mother is so she can eat you."

Kaylee looked back at Parker and shook her head with disappointment.

On the other side of the jungle, Ryan and Owen scaled the side of a rocky hill in order to get a better lay of the land.

"I've never been much of a rock climber." Owen said to Ryan who was ahead of him. Ryan climbed like a pro.

"It's just like climbing a ladder."

"A ladder that's railings are sharp jagged rocks that crumble under the pressure of your feet."

"You know Owen, this is the dream world. You can give yourself massive triceps so you don't have to struggle so much. Or..." A rope unfurled from the top of the cliff. "You could use a rope." Ryan grasped the rope and used it to walk up the side of the rock wall horizontally. "Yeah, this is much easier."

"So is this." Owen said, speeding past Ryan in a glass elevator.

"The least you could've done was come up with something that looked prehistoric. You're ruining the ancient ambiance."

Within moments, the shiny brass railings that Owen was gripping de-evolved into dried brown vines, and the elevator's pulley system turned into a rope attached to a large rock that used Earth's gravity to hurl him upward.

Jolting to a stop at the top of the wood pulley system the vine swung violently as Owen held it with all of his mite. "Not cool Ryan."

Ryan couldn't help but laugh at the look of terror on his friends' face.

Ryan leapt from his elevator vine to the hill top as Ryan neared the top, and then Owen helped heave Ryan to the surface.

"We're here. Now what?"

Ryan looked out at the land and had to sit down to take it all in. "Look at that!"

Owen followed Ryan's gaze and found himself dazed as well. The land was flatter than they expected. Watery mudflats shimmered on the ground reflecting the colorful sky above. The setting sun produced pink and purple hues, mixed with blue and white. They saw how the jungle expanded outward to the west and a dryer, volcanic looking, rocky area dotted across the east. Directly in front of them, they saw a substantial gathering of dinosaurs gathered around a watering hole.

Pterodactyls circled in the sky, as their large shadows trailed over the ground. Brontosaurus's stood as tall as nearby trees and stretched their long necks out, shaking their heads like they were swatting away flies.

Just then there was a rumbling on the ground. The nearby dinosaurs lifted their heads from the water and turned to face the sound. The rumbling of the ground continued, followed by an awful screeching sound. Ryan and Owen could barely hear the high pitched sounds of human screams.

Ryan turned to Owen, "Blake!"

"Justin!" Owen countered.

The noise and earth tremors continued to grow and the nearby dinosaurs took off running. The pterodactyls in the sky screeched and flew away.

"A T-Rex must be after them!"

"We've got to save them."

They watched as smaller dinosaurs ran out of the volcanic valley as if they were being chased. Kaylee and Parker ran up to Ryan and Owen, out of breath.

"Blake and Justin?" Kaylee asked.

"That's our guess."

"We've got to help them!"

"They sound like they're not gonna make it."

Just then a loud, *Aarghhhh* erupted out of the cavern. Whatever it was, it was getting closer. The four didn't know what to expect but Owen was making plans to run away.

Just then a giant Tyrannosaurus Rex burst out from behind the cavern wall and spun on its heels wildly. Its gigantic green tail swung around violently. The four ducked to miss it. Its head and upper torso bent down toward the ground. He spun up like a tornado.

Just then, it tripped over its own tail, and stumbled to the ground, and slid on its chin knocking up a large cloud of dust.

When the dust cloud settled, the four onlookers couldn't believe their eyes.

Blake and Justin were holding onto a large vine wrapped around the T-Rex's neck. They were so small in comparison to the T-Rex, the four missed them at first.

"Woohoo!" Blake leapt to his feet on top of the giant dinosaurs back. "That was sensational!"

"Best eight-second ride ever!" Justin exclaimed.

The others were laughing until another loud rumbling caught their attention. They all looked up as a flaming fireball smashed to the ground. "Asteroid!!!" Kaylee screamed as the others joined in.

"We're gonna die with the dinosaurs!" Owen cried.

"Everyone back to the time machine! Run, run!"

Running as fast as they could, they leapt for the machine like they were sliding to home base. They were piled on top of each other in a heap of arms and legs, when Kaylee screamed "Present time!"

As their time machine ball rolled to a stop, the six un tangled themselves and finally caught their breath and slowed their pounding hearts. After some deep sighs of relief, they each started laughing.

"That was so close!"

"I can't believe you harnessed a T-Rex!"

"I can't believe we nearly became extinct!" They climbed out of the time machine and crawled onto the green grass. They sat there, soaking in the warmth of the sun, the fresh cool breeze and the aroma of wildflowers.

"Anyone else hungry? I'm thinking pizza cake and gum drop pie!"

Chapter 23

For days, the kids had adventure after adventure. They tried everything anyone had ever thought of and went back to try it again later. They ate like pigs, played like monkeys and flew like birds. They even became animals to see what it was like and then learned each other's languages. From oink to moo, neigh and roar, they mastered every animal language and then created pop songs with the animal lyrics and watched as their once human crowd of fans became the animal world. Two by two, like Noah's Ark, the children watched as every animal known to man (and a few we hadn't discovered yet) appeared and introduced themselves.

Kaylee learned why unicorns can't be seen and Justin befriended a few dodo birds, quickly learning why they, like the dinosaurs, were extinct. (It didn't have anything to do with asteroids this time, though.)

Finally, at the end of day four, Kaylee decided she needed to bring in some books so they could learn more so they could design new adventures. The boys decided they'd rather enter the books instead and have those adventures instead of reading about them. Day five was filled with Tom Sawyer, Swiss Family Robinson, The Magic Tree House, Star Wars and about three dozen different comic books.

As day six approached, their brains were tapped. Between the six of them, they had done everything they could think of, sometimes twice and they couldn't think of anything more. They sat around rubbing their bellies full of ice cream and cake, resting on their floating rainbow hammocks and getting back rubs from green monkeys when Kaylee finally broke the silence.

"I think we need to go home."

"What?" The boys groaned.

"We can't think of anything else to do. We need to go home and go back to school and learn more so we can have more adventures."

"Can't we learn here? Without classrooms and tests?"

"And parents with rules like clean your room and put away your laundry?"

"I don't think so," Kaylee began, "think about it. Every story we went into we either read in class or from a book at the library.

"Or saw on TV or at the movies..."

Kaylee continued. "Every adventure we had was either from or inspired by something that we learned in the real world. The reason why we don't have anything else to do right now, is because we need to read more stories."

"Or watch more TV!"

Owen had been listening to Kaylee and the others moaning about her suggestion of going home, but he kind of agreed with her. In fact, he was getting a little home sick. "How many days have we been here?"

The guys looked up at him with inquisitive looks.

"Just a night."

"Uh-uh," Blake shook his head no, "We've been here for like a week. Think about how many times we slept."

"How do you know each time we slept it was a real night? The first day the night came to show the fireworks but we made it day again."

"Right, but we weren't sleepy then." Justin added.

"I was." Owen admitted.

"I mean," Justin spoke again, "the times we actually slept were real nights because we were all tired from an entire days worth of adventures."

"Okay, so how many times was that?" Kaylee asked then watched the boys open their hands and start counting on fingers.

"Five."

"Seven."

"Two." Ryan spoke with a smile.

"Two?" Justin scoffed, you didn't sleep the other nights when we slept?"

"Why would I? I just sped time ahead until you all woke up." He grinned as he pulled out the universal remote he had made.

Kaylee was now incredibly confused. "If you sped time, do those nights count?"

"Of course they don't." Blake spoke. "That would mean we've been here since the creation of the universe, to the end of the world and back again."

"No, no. Those were just adventures. They don't count."

"Don't they?"

Everyone stared at each other. With eyes wide and shrugging shoulders, no one knew what to make of this.

"Maybe it's just been one night then." Kaylee suggested.

"How do you figure?"

"We would have woken up if morning would have arrived."

"I don't know," Blake spoke, "I once slept an entire Saturday and most of Sunday before I woke up."

"Really? Your parents let you sleep that long?" Kaylee asked curiously.

Blake shrugged his shoulders.

"Doesn't matter," Ryan added, "we want to wake up now, so let's do it."

"Great." Parker stood and clapped his hands together. "How do we leave?"

Ryan looked at everyone staring at him. They continued to stare until he felt really nervous. He didn't have a trick or anything.

"Ryan, how do we wake up?"

Ryan shrugged his shoulders. "I dunno. The sun comes up."

"The sun has come up many times, we haven't woken up."

"Actually, we have. We were asleep in the dream world."

"So make the sun come up while we are awake."

"I'm pretty sure if you want it to happen, it makes it a dream, so it won't be the real sun rising."

"Why can't we just want to wake up and do it?"

"Just like you want an ice cream cone..."

"No more ice cream." Parker groaned still holding his expanded tummy.

"Well I want to wake up." Kaylee spoke, "and it's not happening."

"Maybe we all have to want to wake up." Justin suggested.

"Well I want to." Owen spoke.

"Me too." Ryan added. The others nodded their heads.

"Okay, so we all want to wake up... but we're still here."

"Maybe we need to think really hard about it?" Kaylee suggested and Ryan and Owen both close their eyes tight and made faces like they were straining to go to the bathroom.

Blake started laughing at them, "You two look ridiculous. What are you doing?"

"Thinking." They said in unison.

"Jinx – you owe me a soda." Just then a can of soda appeared in Parker's hand. "Thanks!"

Chapter 24

The six of them continued arguing and trying to come up with ways to wake up to no avail. Days went by. On day nine, panic set in.

"Our parents are bound to be beside themselves!" Owen cried.

"What do you mean?" Parker asked.

"Think about it. We've been here for nine days now! We've missed a week of school AND a weekend! I was supposed to go to Splash Town with my cousin."

"Do you really think we've been asleep for that long? Why wouldn't our parents have woken us up?"

"I know my mom, never would have let me sleep through a day of school. "Kaylee spoke certainly.

"How do we know it has really been as long as we think? Maybe it's just been a couple of hours in the real world."

"Yeah, well maybe it's been a week and we are all next to each other in the hospital in coma's completely baffling the doctors who can't get us to wake up?!" Kaylee added.

"Comas?" Blake repeated. "Like near dead?"

"You don't think they'd think we we're dead, do you?"

"We'd still be breathing." Kaylee confirmed.

"I'll bet my parents would have taken me to the hospital."

"Mine too."

"So we are all lined up in a hospital room, hooked up to feeding tubes and machines and our parents are sitting there crying, worried sick about us because we can't wake up!"

"That's horrible!"

"Why have you done this to us Ryan?" Kaylee cried.

"Me?" Ryan fired back, "It was your idea to do this."

"Yeah!" Justin and Blake both screamed.

"I didn't know this was going to happen. How could I?"

"You're the smart one."

"You ALL are smart."

"Especially Parker." Blake envisioned Parker's glasses back on his face.

"Why did I get these back?"

"You look smarter with them on and we need smart right now."

"I'm pretty sure the glasses don't determine my Intelligence Quotient."

"See, you just used three long words in one sentence, you're already smarter. Now think of a way to get us out of here!"

"I can't. I hardly know how to control my dreams. Not like Ryan."

Just then everyone turned to Ryan again. He groaned. "This has never happened before but we should be able to figure it out."

"Someone pinch him." Parker ordered. Owen pinched him.

"Ouch, why did you do that?"

"Isn't that what you do to wake up?"

"I don't know. But it didn't work."

Just then Blake punched him in the arm.

"Oww!"

"I just wanted to be certain."

Before long, everyone was trying to pinch, scream and scare each other awake. They failed.

They sat on the grass glaring at each other when Justin had an epiphany.

"Ah ha!" He screeched making everyone jump. "I've got it!"

"What?"

"I'm the key."

"How do you figure?"

"I'm the only one who can force myself to wake up."

They all stared at him curiously.

"When I'm falling I wake up before I hit the ground."

"But now, you know you won't die."

"It's still scary enough to wake me."

"Good idea." Blake stood and mentally created a mountain right where they stood. The ground shot up in jagged points, higher and higher into the sky until they all stood on the edge of a cliff with Justin right at the ledge.

"What are you doing?" Kaylee asked.

"Justin has to fall. He can't do it from the ground." Blake answered.

"If he jumps off the cliff, he will know he is fine because he will be prepared."

"Then I'll push him."

"You can't do that!" Parker screeched, "what if he falls and dies!"

"You can't die here."

"We also thought we could wake up whenever we wanted, but look how that turned out."

"This will work, as long as I don't know it's coming." Justin persisted.

"You are standing on the ledge discussing it. I don't see how you won't know it's coming. Maybe I should give you amnesia!"

"If you do that, he might not remember he needs to wake up before he dies."

"I have to be the one." Justin cut in. "I have to fall, hopefully not to my death, so I can wake up. Then I can find you guys and wake you up once I am out in the real world. It's the only way.

"I still don't like the idea." Ryan wished he knew more about the dream world than he did. "But I think Justin is right. I can't think of anything else."

"But what if he dies?"

"We could just stay here." Parker offered.

"No we can't." Kaylee spoke surely. "If we don't wake up, we could starve to death in the real world."

"Not if we're hooked up to feeding tubes."

"You want to stay like that for the rest of your life?"

"I'm cool with it."

"Well I'm not!" Blake shouted. With a leap on his feet he lunged towards Justin and pushed him with all of his might. Justin flew backwards, over the edge, screaming. He looked at Blake as he fell from view.

"Wake up!" Blake yelled aloud as Ryan and Owen tackled him to the ground.

"What did you do?"

"You just killed him!"

"I didn't kill him – I saved US!"

Kaylee ran to the cliff's edge and looked over, watching Justin fall. He was screaming with pure terror. A megaphone appeared in her hands, "Wake up!" she yelled into it.

Justin kept screaming. The ground was nearing. He was terrified. Kaylee could see the blind terror in his eyes. "This has to work." She whispered as she kept staring, praying, hoping. She prepared herself for the splat. He was so close to the ground now. It would only be another second or two. If Justin was going to escape it would have to be now. "Any second, any second..."

Then before her very eyes, as fast as a blink, Justin was gone. No splat. Just gone.

"He's gone!" She screamed.

"He's dead?" Owen nearly cried.

"No! He's gone. He's gone to the other side."

"Heaven?"

Parker fell to his knees and wailed, throwing his arms up to the sky. "Why? Why my dear friend?"

Kaylee's face expressed a dumbfounded annoyance so extreme Owen was certain her hair was turning grey.

"The real world." She stood, motioning outward with her hands. "He's back in the real world."

"Then why hasn't he woken us up yet?"

"He just got there. Give him time."

"How much time?"

"He's got to wake up. Remember the dream. Then call us."

"What if he doesn't remember his dream?"

"We've remembered them in the past."

"Not all of them. There've been many mornings I wake up and can't remember dreaming. What if that happens to Justin?"

"Then he'll figure it out when we don't show up in school."

"What if it's still the weekend? It'd be days before he gets back to school."

Kaylee was seconds from pulling her own hair out of her head. "We've just got to be patient, and hope."

"Great!" Parker mumbled. "Our fates depend on a kid who spent years thinking he was going to die whenever he fell asleep."

Chapter 25

"Ahhhhhhhh!" Justin screamed as he fell out of bed and hit his bedroom floor with a thud. He opened his eyes and looked around frantically. *What happened?* He wondered as his eyes grew accustomed to the dark. Finally realizing he was home and had fallen out of bed, he remembered he had been dreaming. Then it all came rushing back to him.

"My friends! They're still trapped in the dream world!" Wiping sweat from his forehead with the back of his hand, he leapt to his feet wondering what day it was.

As he raced out of his bedroom and down the hall to the telephone, his adrenaline was peeked. He ran into the kitchen, flicked on the light and startled his father.

"Justin! What are you doing?" He demanded as he put his sandwich back down on a plate.

"Ryan, Owen, Parker, Blake and Kaylee – they're trapped in the other world. I need to call and wake them up."

"Oh, no you're not."

"But I have to! If I don't wake them up, they are going to stay asleep!"

"That's the idea son."

"But we've been asleep for over a week! How have you not noticed?"

"It's only been four hours, son."

"Really?" Justin was astonished.

"Yes."

"All of that happened in only four hours?"

"What happened? Did you have a dream?"

"The craziest dream ever!"

"Well you can tell me about it in the morning."

"But Dad, I promised to call them."

"You shouldn't make promises you know you can't keep. And you aren't calling anyone this late at night! Go back to bed."

"But dad!"

"Don't but me, you shouldn't even be up right now."

Justin's brain clicked into gear. "Why are *you* up, Dad?" Justin asked, looking quizzically at his father and his massive ham sandwich sitting on the counter. His father stuttered, attempting to come up with something to say. "Don't worry dad, I won't tell mom, if..."

Curious, his father bit. "What do you want?"

"To make a phone call."

"No can do, son. Your friend's parents would never forgive me."

Justin realized his father was right. It would be their parents that answered the phone, not his friends. And the parents wouldn't believe him or wake up their children. He'd have to wait until morning, whether he wanted to or not. His head drooped. "Yes, Dad."

As Justin sat in bed he couldn't help but think of his friends, stuck there in that world for another, how many days? He started wondering how long it would be, how long had it been? Since it was only one in the morning there was another six hours before he could call to wake them up.

To his friends it would be another week or more before they could escape the dream world. They'd think he forgot about them. He failed them. Would they ever forgive him? Now, he was afraid to sleep! Instead of a fear of falling, he now had a fear of returning to the dream world and facing his angry friends. Would they believe it had only been a few hours? Justin pulled out a book to read so he could stay awake. It was a long, long night as he watched the minutes tick by as slow as a snail racing a turtle.

As the sun began to rise, the dark circles under his eyes were back. Like a zombie searching for brains, he groggily made his way to the kitchen. His parents were still in bed. Granted it was only about 6:30 in the morning on a Sunday, but he expected them to wake up soon.

He sat at the counter on a stool and waited. Plopping his chin on his fist and leaning on his elbow, he waited. About twenty minutes later his mother emerged from the bedroom and headed to the kitchen to start a pot of coffee.

"What are you doing up so early?" She asked as she filled the coffee pot.

"When can I call Parker and Ryan?"

"It's way too early to call. You'll wake them up. You should wait until at least eight."

"That's two days away!" Justin groaned.

"That's an hour away, and what's up with the attitude, mister?"

"They've been waiting for me to call all night!"

"I'm certain they will understand."

"I'm not." Justin muttered.

"Would you like to talk about it?"

Justin thought about telling her. Talking might help, but would his mother even understand? "Nah. It's okay." He decided his mom would think he was either insane or completely making it up.

"Well then, would you like some breakfast while you wait? It'll make the time fly by faster."

"Okay."

"Good." She pulled bacon and eggs from the refrigerator.

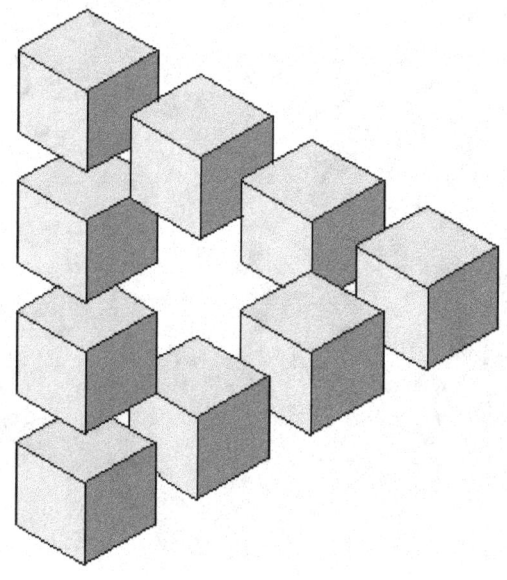

Chapter 26

At about 8:45, Justin was zoned out in front of the TV when his father walked into the living room. "Time to mow the lawn, son."

"What?"

"Don't pretend you didn't hear me. You agreed to mow the lawn for a month in exchange for that video game I bought you."

"What time is it?" Justin began to panic, suddenly remembering his friends.

"A quarter till nine."

"Oh my gosh! I forgot about them!"

"Who?"

"My friends. I should have called them an hour ago!"

"Guess you shouldn't have wasted time watching TV then."

"But I had to do something while I waited for the time to pass."

"And it did. The day is wasting away."

"But Dad, I've got to make a phone call first."

"No sir. You've got chores to do. You can play with your friends when you're done."

"But Dad!"

"That's the second 'but Dad' I've heard from you," his father said sternly. "You don't want to go for a third."

Justin knew his father was getting angry. He knew that a third time meant three strikes and you're out, and he knew he never wanted to find out what his father's *out* was. He didn't like getting grounded, and that is most likely where it would lead.

He dropped his head and reluctantly lifted himself from the couch.

While mowing the lawn, all Justin could think about was his friends and how they were probably still stuck in the dream world. Would their parents be worried about them if they hadn't woken up by now? Would they think their children were ill and needed the rest or would they try to wake them up? Would they call 911? Would they think their children were stuck in a coma? Would the doctors know what to do? What tests would they run? Would the tests hurt? Justin could save them that devastation if he could just make a phone call.

He was half done mowing the lawn when he decided he HAD to make that call, grounding or not.

He turned off the lawn mower and snuck into the house. He reached for the phone and dialed a number. He heard the first ring when his father walked into the room.

"What exactly are you doing?"

"I have to make this call!"

"The only thing you have to do is the lawn. Now hang up that phone."

"But Dad!"

"Strike three." His father growled as he took the phone and hung it up just as Ryan's mother answered.

"You don't understand, Dad. It's imperative that I call them."

"Good use of the word imperative." His mother said as she walked into the room. "What's going on?"

"Your son thinks play comes before work."

"Work before play, Justin. You know the rules."

"But Mom, I…"

Two hours later, Justin found himself alone, tired and grounded in his room. He worried all day, all night and eagerly awaited the morning so he could get to school and see if his friends were there.

Chapter 27

As Justin exited the bus, he wondered what he would find. Would his friends be at school? Would they be angry? Would they be absent? If they were absent, would that mean they were in comas at the hospital?

As he made his way down the hall, his heart began beating violently in his chest. He could feel his ribcage rattle. He could even hear himself breathing. He was so nervous, he was nearly sick to his stomach. He wished he hadn't eaten breakfast because now it was kicking him in the gut!

He walked up to his locker, turned and looked around. He waited to see if anyone showed up. He waited and waited. Looking over the crowd of students, between the bodies, he saw no one familiar. He saw many faces he recognized, but none of them were his friends from the dream world.

The bell rang.

As he made his way to class, a rock the size of an elephant weighed on his shoulders. His stomach churned.

If none of his friends were in class; that meant the worst; they were stuck in the dream world.

As he walked into class, he saw almost all of the seats were filled - all except his friends' seats. He slumped down miserably in the chair of his desk, feeling sick.

The teacher walked in and took roll call, marking Ryan, Owen, Parker, Blake and Kaylee absent. Justin groaned loudly.

"Justin, are you feeling alright?" The teacher asked.

Justin wanted to disappear. He felt like such a failure. He had failed his friends! It was all his fault, but what could he tell the teacher? Phone calls during school hours were not allowed. He frowned.

"I'm fine, Mrs. James. I'm sorry."

"Okay." She sang as she put the roster on her desk and began speaking to the class. "Students please pull out your notepads and a pencil. We are having a pop quiz."

This time it was the class's turn to groan. If Justin could have felt any worse he would have, but all he could think about was his lost friends.

The pop quiz was passed back to him, and as he looked down at the paper he couldn't seem to focus on the questions. How could he? He was so distraught over his friends. Lost in thought, he imagined the hospital room his friends must all be laying in. He couldn't help but wonder what the doctors were thinking. Were they running tests? Brain scans? Would they find anything they could do?

Before Justin knew it, class was over and he hadn't filled out a single answer. He groaned as he stood, turned in his empty test and walked out the door.

School was a complete haze. He couldn't remember anything that actually happened. It was as if he were so consumed with his failure, nothing else mattered.

Finally school was released and Justin made it back home.

"How was your day son?" His mother asked.

"Horrible!"

"Why?"

"I feel sick. Absolutely horrible!"

His mother reached over and felt his forehead with the back of her hand. "You don't feel hot?"

Justin looked at her inquisitively and then suddenly an idea popped into his head. Why hadn't he thought about this earlier? It was genius!

"Ohhh! He groaned loudly as he held his stomach."

"Justin! What's wrong?"

"I'm dying! I've got to go to the hospital!"

"Was it something you ate?"

"Oh, ohhh!" Justin groaned again. His stomach had hurt all day, so it wasn't a complete lie. If he could get his mom to take him to the hospital, then he could go find his friends and wake them.

"Where does it hurt?" His mother asked as she poked at his sides, apparently worried about his appendix.

"Everywhere." Justin spoke, feeling more sick now about lying. His mom was in panic mode and she grabbed her purse.

Would this work? Would she take him to the hospital? Would he be given a shot? Would they want to operate? How would he get away and how would he find his friends?

Chapter 28

The drive to the hospital was a painful one. Every time Justin thought about the worry he was causing his mother, his stomach hurt more, and he groaned.

"We'll be there in a couple more minutes." She spoke in a panic.

His mom rushed him into the emergency room and, as Justin entered, and smelled the distinct odor of disinfectant and hospital people, his stomach ached again on its own. "Ohh!" He groaned.

His mom spoke to a nurse who led Justin to a private room where she asked him to undress and put on a hospital gown. As he undressed, he wondered just how far he was going to have to take this charade? How was he going to get out of here? How was he going to find his friends? They could be anywhere.

Just then, he heard two doctors talking just on the other side of the dividing curtain.

"Any luck?"

"It's the strangest thing I've ever seen. There doesn't seem to be any physical connection between the five except they are all showing the same symptoms..."

This had to be his friends they were talking about. Justin leaned in to listen closer.

"I've requested MRI's be performed on each of them. I've got a team heading to the 4th floor to get them right now."

Fourth floor! Justin raced out of the curtained room only to run into his mom and a doctor.

"Where are you going young man?"

"I've got to go! There's no time!"

Justin's mom reached for him, but he squirmed out of her grasp and ran off. He hadn't realized she had grabbed his hospital gown until he made his way into the waiting room. Everyone turned and started laughing. He looked down to find he was standing there in nothing but his Spiderman underwear.

Wanting to scream, wanting to throw up, and wanting to disappear, Justin just turned and ran down the hall. He ducked into the first patient room that was open. Inside the room, he heard the beep of a heart monitor as he saw an elderly man sleeping on the bed. He noticed a bathrobe on the back of the chair and grabbed it.

Starting out of the room, he paused, hearing the hustle of a couple orderlies and his mom racing down the hall looking for him. He waited until the coast was clear then tiptoed back down the hall to the elevators.

Once inside the elevator he pressed the fourth floor button and exhaled a sigh of relief. His stomach was still in knots, but knowing he was getting closer to his friends made him feel a little better.

With a ding, the elevator stopped on the fourth floor and the doors slid open. The hallway was dark and deep. It seemed to stretch out in front of him a mile long. As he made his way down the hall it seemed to stretch farther and farther. He began to run, harder and faster, making his way down the hall as it continued to stretch. As he finally approached the two double doors, he noticed guards standing on either side.

"Where do you think you're going, young man?"

"My friends. I think they're in there."

"That area is quarantined. No one in, no one out."

"Why?"

"We have five children, all in comas, for no apparent reason. The CDC needs to rule out infectious disease."

"They're not sick. They're dreaming. If I could just go in there, I could wake them."

"What makes you think you can wake them when the doctors and their parents haven't been able to?"

"I have to. I was sent to wake them."

"By who?"

"By them, of course."

The guards exchanged curious glances. One reached for his radio, and the other reached for Justin. "Listen kid, we're going to have to hold you here…"

Realizing he was facing another obstacle, his stomach began to hurt again. When he doubled over holding his belly, the guards changed their tune.

"Kid, are you okay? Should we get someone?"

A guard went over to get a chair for Justin while the other walked toward the nurse's station for assistance. With the guards distracted, Justin made his move. He wriggled through the doors of the quarantine area and raced down the hall.

He could hear the guards calling for backup, but found that they weren't following him. They were afraid of whatever it was that held his friends in captive sleep. They didn't want to pick up their disease.

Scanning the patient door windows, he quickly found his friends' room and pushed his way through the doors.

Seeing his friends laying there, seemingly lifeless with breathing tubes and chords and cables hooked to blinking, beeping monitors was frightening. But Justin knew exactly what he had to ... didn't he?

First, he ran to Ryan and shook him by the shoulders. "Ryan! Ryan wake up!" Ryan didn't stir.

He ran to Owen and shook him. He picked him up by the shoulders and yelled in his ear, but when Owen didn't wake, Justin let him flop back down on his pillow.

"Kaylee! You've got to wake up! He saw a book laying next to her on the bedside table. He grabbed it, flipped it open half way and then slammed it closed as loud as he could. No response.

Justin panicked. He stood in the middle of the room and yelled at the top of his lungs, "Guys! You have to wake up! Wake up!! Wake up!!!"

Everyone was still asleep. No one moved at all. Not even the slightest eyelid flutter.

Just then Justin's mother walked in followed by a doctor, and the guards. "What's going on here?" His mother asked. "I know these children."

"They have been unconscious since Saturday morning. We've tried everything, but haven't been able to wake them up." The doctor explained.

"Why? What's wrong with them?"

"That's what I have been trying to tell you." Justin spoke up. "They are trapped in the dream world, and only I can save them."

"How can you save them, Justin?" His mom asked.

Justin turned to look back at his friends. He was here. He was with them. He was awake. He had tried shaking them. He'd tried screaming... He ran to Blake and punched his shoulder. Nothing. He punched his shoulder again, "Come on, Blake. Wake up!"

The doctor spoke. "No one can wake them up. There is nothing that we can do. We must let them go."

"Let them go? Justin asked with pure panic in his voice. "What do you mean?!"

174

"We are going to have to pull the plug. It's been three days. We've got to let them pass."

Chapter 29

"No!!" Justin yelled. He ran to Ryan and picked him up from his pillow. "Wake up Ryan, wake up!" He screamed in his face and then slapped him on the cheek.

"Justin!" His mother scolded as the guards approached to restrain him. He scampered under their grasps and ran to Parker's bed. He leaped on top of the boy and began shaking him, bouncing his head on his pillow. "You've got to wake up, now!"

The guards grabbed Justin's arms and heaved him off of the sleeping boy. Justin thrashed trying to free himself from the guards clutches as he watched the doctor, listen to Ryan's heartbeat through a stethoscope. The doctor shook his head sadly, and Justin's mother began to cry.

"No! You can't do it!" Justin hollered as the doctor reached for the electric plug that powered Ryan's machine. "You can't do it! You'll kill them!"

The guards dragged Justin from the room. He was so upset, so afraid. A sharp pain cut through his stomach. The room blurred as he squirmed in the guards' grasp. Tripping over their feet, Justin fell.

The room went dark and though Justin should have landed on the floor with a smack, the tile disappeared and Justin found himself falling down, down, down.

He fell from space and time, passing by stars, asteroids and spaceships firing green lasers. He fell into the atmosphere of the dream world and through the clouds into the waters of the sea and into the belly of the beast where he was spit out screaming and landed on the gym floor surrounded by his friends.

Screaming in a panic, Justin finally opened his eyes to see the worried faces of his five friends all looking down at him.

"Justin! Man, are you okay?"

"You're awake!"

"Of course we're awake. We're just glad *you're* awake."

"Me?" He questioned as he tried to sit up. "Oh my stomach!" He groaned as he reached for his upset belly.

"Are you okay? Blake got you pretty good with the ball."

"The ball?" Justin asked with complete confusion.

"Yeah, we were playing dodge ball just now and Blake got you good. You caught the ball square in the center of your gut and flew backwards like five feet, skidding to a stop, hitting your head on the floor and passing out. We were worried about you."

"How long have I been out?"

"Just a few minutes. Why?"

"Minutes? It's been days!" Justin sat up quick, his head spinning.

The others glanced at each other then looked back at Justin. "Dude, are you okay?"

"I don't understand. We were all in the dream world but then Blake pushed me off a cliff and I woke up, but I wasn't allowed to call and wake you all up, and I got grounded."

The group stared at him dumbly.

"Then I had to find a way to get to the hospital to wake you, but they were going to pull the plug on you and let you die."

"It sounds like you had a really weird dream." Owen spoke.

"Are you serious? That whole thing was a dream?" Justin sat there in confusion.

179

Ryan shook his head. "Actually, it sounds like you had a false awakening."

"A false awakening? What's that?" Justin and Kaylee both asked in unison.

"A false awakening happens when you have a lucid dream - when you are aware you are dreaming. You think you wake up and go through your day like normal only to find you are still dreaming and wake up again."

Justin thought about that for a couple seconds. "How do I know I am not still dreaming?"

"Well we are here aren't we?"

"Yeah?"

"And you know why your stomach hurts now, right?"

"Yeah?" Justin sat there thinking. "But that means I was having a lucid dream BEFORE I woke up."

Just then Owen cupped his hand to his mouth and spoke through his fingers. "Uh-oh."

"What's wrong, Owen?" Kaylee asked.

"I just lost a tooth." He lowered his hand to show everyone the tooth. "I think I'm still dreaming."

"Maybe you really did just lose a tooth. These things happen." Parker suggested.

Owen didn't buy it. He looked at Justin with fear in his eyes. If Justin were still sleeping and Owen was still sleeping, then that must mean that everyone else was still sleeping. But where were they? Were they in the safety of their beds or being monitored in a hospital? And when was it? Was it still Friday night? And how on earth would they wake up if they all were still asleep?

Justin looked over at Kaylee, who looked over at Blake, who looked at Parker who looked to Ryan. Ryan, the one who could control his dreams, the one who started all of this, the one, the only one who could save them, knew it was up to him. He must determine if they were all still dreaming.

As he looked back at his friends, they smiled at him. They may have been afraid but they also trusted Ryan. Through all of this, all of their super adventures they had become the best of friends. Friends that Ryan could share his dreams with – he was no longer alone. This made him smile.

Ryan looked around the gym. They had all just been playing dodge ball. It all seemed so real, but lucid dreams *did* seem real and false awakenings did as well.

Ryan took a deep breath and looked up to the ceiling, glanced back at the expectant faces of his friends and smiled. He knew what he could do to answer their question – are we awake or asleep?

He exhaled, closed his eyes, lifted his arms above his head and willed himself to fly.

The End...

...Or is it?

Finish the story...

Using your own imagination,
what do you think could happen next?

Is Ryan going to take off from the floor and start flying around the gym, where everyone suddenly realizes they are still asleep?

Is Ryan going to press off from the floor only to realize he can't fly and that everyone is awake and it really is all over?

Or...

Has Ryan had a false awakening as well? Does he think he is awake and therefore can't fly? What could happen later in the dream to help them realize they are still asleep?

As you can see the story can go in multiple different directions. It could be over, it could continue and that continuation could be as crazy or as simple as you imagine it to be.

Hello. My name is Kathleen and I am the author of this story. The purpose of this section is to encourage you to use your imagination. When I visit schools and talk with students, one of the things I always make sure to tell them is that **Writing is 100% imagination**. The greatest thing about story telling is that you can *BE* anyone YOU want, *GO* anywhere YOU dream, and *DO* anything YOU wish. You are not limited by your situation, location or financial status.

When I was your age, riding the school bus, I would stare out the window and imagine myself flying. I would soar over buildings, fly between cars, chase bad guys and save the planet during that long half hour drive to and from school. That is where this story came from; my imagination. And with your imagination, this story can continue.

While I always want to encourage you to write down your thoughts and ideas, you don't have to. If you use pencil and paper or a computer, the stories will always be there for you, long after you've forgotten this story, but if you just use your imagination, there is nothing wrong with that. The purpose is to have fun with it.

Now you may ask; I don't know how to write a story, how do I start? You start with an idea; in this case, are they awake or not? And then you ask one simple question – over and over again – What happens next?

What Happens Next? THIS is one of the most important questions an author asks him or herself. No matter how far you get in the story, how stuck you are, all you need to do is ask, what happens next and imagine what you would do next if you were in that situation.

Think about scenario 3. Ryan tries to take off but can't. He assumes they are awake. He tells everyone, nope, we're awake, but what if you believe they ARE still asleep? What happens next? What is going to happen to show them they are still asleep? Maybe a giant vulture flies in through the window and grabs Blake and takes him off to feed the baby birds? Maybe they all walk out into the hallway after class to discover the hallway is a long tunnel leading to an alternate reality where students run the school and teachers take the tests. What would convince YOU, that you were still asleep? What wild and crazy adventure could YOU come up with?

What Happens Next? If something absolutely crazy happened, how would they fix it? How would they get out of that mess? How would they wake up? And once they did wake up, would it be Saturday morning or Monday at school? Would they wake up in the hospital and how much time has passed? Would they be old, with white hair and wrinkles?

The Only Limitation
is Your Own Imagination!

So, take some time. Write your own story. Have your own adventures. Then, maybe, when you've written something that is so totally cool you'll want to share with others... you might consider publishing it.

That is what it is to be a writer. That IS creative writing. Writing class doesn't have to be boring when WHAT you write, can lead you to the stars.

HAVE FUN WITH IT!

About the Author

Kathleen J. Shields is an award-winning author having won first place from the Texas Association of Authors for "Hamilton Troll meets Dinosaurs". The Hamilton Troll Adventure series is educational and inspirational, teaching young children social skills, animal characteristics and how to handle real-life situations.

Shields' also runs a website and graphic design company called Kathleen's Graphics. She designs colorful, eye-catching websites, logos and advertisements for businesses, entrepreneurs and authors. She thoroughly enjoys being challenged to learn new things to make her client's websites and her own, top notch.

She also runs the Erin Go Bragh publishing company and has published various books; from fully-illustrated rhyming stories for ages 4 and up, children's chapter books for ages 8 and up, and young adult stories and situations. Her objective with Erin Go Bragh is to promote literacy and education through writing.

Additionally, Kathleen writes an inspirational and educational blog regarding her endeavors as an author as well as a business woman and Christian. Her views are always light-hearted and thought-provoking and are intended to get the reader thinking.

For more information about the author,
and her books, please visit:

www.KathleensBooks.com

or follow her blog at

kathleenjshields.wordpress.com

www.ingramcontent.com/pod-product-compliance
Lightning Source LLC
Chambersburg PA
CBHW051512170626
46811CB00002B/784